WITNESS

She was the woman he loved and he would save her.
Even if it cost him his life ...

Detective John Book froze.

Police Chief Schaeffer was holding his pistol to
Rachel's head, and he said, 'Drop it, Johnny, or I'll
blow her head into small pieces.'

Book, still holding the empty shotgun, dropped it.
And said, 'Schaeffer, you hurt her, I'll peel you like a
grape.'

At that moment there came the sound of a bell,
clanging rapidly, from the direction of the main house.
Then, out of the woodlands, they came, at a trot or a
steady walk ... the Amish. Dozens of them. All
coming to answer the sound of the bell, the Amish cry
for help.

WITNESS

William Kelley and Earl W. Wallace

Based on the screenplay by
Earl W. Wallace and William Kelley

NEW ENGLISH LIBRARY

First published in the U.S.A. in 1985 by Pocket Books, a division of Simon & Schuster, Inc.

First NEL Paperback Edition April 1985
Reprinted May 1985

NEL Books are published by
New English Library,
Mill Road, Dunton Green,
Sevenoaks, Kent.
Editorial office: 47 Bedford Square, London WC1B 3DP

Printed and bound in Great Britain by
Cox & Wyman Ltd, Reading

British Library C.I.P.

Kelley, William
  Witness.
  I. Title II. Wallace, Earl
  813′.54[F]   PS3561.E39

ISBN 0 450 05863 8

PROLOGUE

CHAPTER ONE

The preacher had begun with John: 5 ("Marvel not at this: for the hour is coming, in which all that are in the graves shall hear his voice, and they shall come forth.") and now, an hour later, he had worked his way out, quotation by quotation, to the twentieth chapter of Revelation. "And the sea gave up the dead which were in it," he chanted, "and death and hell delivered up the dead which were in them: and they were judged every man according to their works."

Rachel Lapp, seated on a straight chair facing the coffin, her back to the preacher, listened closely and tried to take solace from the preacher's words. An Amish funeral was supposed to be a celebration of sorts. Another Christian victory. But Rachel had sometimes found the spirit of the thing a bit difficult to summon up. Even when the decedent had lived a long and happy life, as was so often the case among the Amish, dead was still dismal as far as Rachel was concerned, and no amount of preachment could redress it.

And on this day the loss was compounded almost beyond endurance. Because the pine coffin—that rough boxful of remains—held all that was mortal of Jacob

Lapp, her husband of barely twelve years. He'd been killed in a farm machine accident, and cut up so badly the coffin would not be opened. A short life, a terrible death, and very difficult, even for the most devout, to celebrate.

"Jacob Lapp," the preacher was saying, "has been called home. Son of Eli, husband of Rachel, father of Samuel . . . he is gone. His voice will be heard no more among us. What are we to say of one taken so young, in the prime of his life? We are to say that God wanted him very much. God's will be done. And we are to take from Jacob's death a warning. You know not the day nor the hour. Be ready for your death, for it comes like a thief in the night."

Rachel glanced down at Samuel, seated next to her, and saw the tears standing in his eyes. And looking to Eli saw the immense sadness in the old man's face. And she thought: How Jacob will miss them, even in heaven. God give Jacob peace.

The first preacher had now finished and taken his seat, and a second preacher—a visitor from Indiana—came forward, and talked some more about death. He addressed himself primarily to those young people who had not yet joined the church. He advised them not to delay lest they die outside the fold. He began to cough after a few minutes, and apologized, saying he had caught a cold on his trip to Lancaster County. He promised to limit his remarks, but coughed his way through thirty more minutes of scriptural quotations and admonitions before he gave the benediction, and yielded the floor.

The first preacher now returned to read the obituary in German. Then, on behalf of the Lapp family, he thanked all those who had been helping out at the farm since Jacob's death, and invited everybody to return to the Lapp house for dinner after the burial. Another minister read the Twenty-third Psalm, and the funeral service was over.

They rode out to the graveyard in their buggies, a long gray line of them, with the horses at a walk and a

9

cold rain falling. The hearse led the procession—a long-bed spring wagon with a black team in the traces—the coffin covered with burlap sacks to protect it from the rain. Eli drove the Lapp buggy directly behind the hearse, staring straight ahead, not speaking until they had left the highway and were following the hearse up the hill into the graveyard.

"So," he said softly. "Not me, but Jacob. Who would believe it?"

Rachel sighed. "Jacob is with God."

The old man nodded, humming for an instant before he spoke. "And very soon I will be with both of them."

"You will live many years yet," Rachel said.

The old man hummed again and shook his head. They were moving now among the tombstones toward where the spring wagon had stopped alongside the open grave. Eli pulled up at the nearest hitching post, climbed down, tethered the horse, then stood stock still looking at the open grave. Rachel took Samuel by the hand, led him straight to the head of the grave, took her stand there, bracing herself against the onslaught of pain.

And painful it was. They brought the coffin over on two hickory poles, set it down upon the grave. Then, as the last of the mourners gathered close around the others, two pallbearers slipped long felt straps around either end of the coffin. The poles were removed, the coffin lowered on the straps into the grave, boards placed over the coffin, and dirt shoveled in until the grave was half full. The rain started to pour down heavily as a minister stepped forward and read a hymn—which hymn Rachel could not make out—stopping frequently as the rainwater flowed off the brim of his hat onto the pages of the hymnbook. He concluded in some confusion, and four pallbearers came forward and finished filling the grave with the rapidly thickening mud.

And through it all Rachel held tight to Samuel's shoulders and let the tears flow down her face with the rain, and prayed to God to receive the gentle soul of

Jacob Lapp into the company of the blessed. For he was a just and good and patient man, she prayed. Especially patient with me, who gave him only one child in twelve years. Who gave him little more in the last ten years but my moods, my excuses, and the cold of my back. Give him warmth now, dear God. Wrap him in the solace of your divine love. And forgive me, God of earth and high heaven, for being neither the wife nor the woman that such a noble and compassionate man so clearly deserved.

When it was over, Rachel had to be helped back to the buggy and into it by Samuel, Eli, and a neighbor by the name of Daniel Hochleitner.

CHAPTER TWO

Rachel watched from the kitchen window as the men—Eli, Samuel, and Daniel Hochleitner—came back up the lane from the county road, all three riding the big wedge-plow behind the team of mules, and all of them, men and mules, steaming at the nostrils in the fifteen-degree afternoon air. She turned and moved the coffeepot over the fire, knowing that they would soon come stomping and blowing through the kitchen door, looking to warm themselves inside and out before the evening chores. She took two pies from the oven, set them to cool by the windows. The men were going out of sight now around the upper barn. She looked away to the pond, to where the waterwheel stood frozen in the ice, and she spoke softly. "I know it is what you would want, Jacob. Daniel was your friend, and he is a good man. But I am not ready to think about another man. Not now, not in a year, maybe not ever. God help me." Then there was the sound of Daniel's voice at the head of the path, and she turned and crossed quickly to the cupboard for cups and saucers, thinking that Jacob had been dead two months and she had yet to visit his grave.

"Momma," Samuel said as he came through the

door, his hands clapped over his ears. "Daniel says if you get your ears froze they fall off."

Rachel put out the cups and saucers, glanced toward Daniel who came through the door wearing a big grin. "Well, if Daniel says so."

"But is it true?" Samuel insisted.

Eli closed the door behind them, walked directly to the stove, his hands extended. "I tell you what is true," he said, huffing. "It's cold enough to freeze the follicles off a brass horse."

"Eli!" Rachel said reprovingly.

"So, follicles?" Eli said, sly-eyed. "It's what the hair comes in."

Rachel turned from him making a small face. "Sit, sit," she said, gesturing Daniel to the table.

"But what about the ears?" said Samuel.

"They don't freeze off," Daniel said, looking somewhat sheepishly at Rachel. "I was fooling."

"Who's fooling?" Eli said, taking his chair at the head of the table. "My ears froze up once, fell right off."

"But you got your ears," Samuel said.

"Sure I do," Eli said. "I stuck them back on with pine tar!"

Eli led the laughter, snuffling into his hot coffee and slapping at the table with his free hand. Daniel, eyeing Rachel in shy glances, hid his smile behind one hand. And Samuel got giggling so fiercely he almost fell off his chair.

Rachel paused at the stove and looked at them fondly. Samuel, laughing, his tousled brown hair swinging about his head, looked so much like his father that it caught at her heart. He had the presence, and the same merry eyes, and the same sweetness in his smile as Jacob, and, for a moment, it stunned her to see the resemblance. And Daniel, smiling delightedly, also reminded her of Jacob. Not so much because of his looks—Daniel wore his hair much longer than Jacob ever did—but because of his spirit, his sense of humor. And, looking at Eli—seeing his great, bearded, patriarchal pleasure in the antics of Samuel and Daniel—she thought: It would be so easy, dear God, this way. So easy to marry Daniel and begin again next spring. A new husband, a happy family, and everybody in the district pleased with my good sense. How easy and how wrong. Oh Lord, save me from easy.

Being Old Order Amish had never been easy for Rachel. Her father, Job Yoder, had been a stern man, a bishop at the time he died. His interpretation of practically everything had been extremely strict. He had refused to allow Rachel's mother, Mary Fisher Yoder, to become involved in the Amish school controversy—even though she had been one of the best school teachers in Lancaster County. He had, in Rachel's opinion, severely restricted her mother, refusing even to permit her to establish an Old Order Amish library (actually a repository for books and historical documents) in Strasburg just before she died.

Her parents and her brother Aaron (then twelve, the baby of the family) had been killed in a truck and buggy accident in Mannheim Township when Rachel was fifteen. A tractor-trailer had crossed the center line, hit the buggy head on at fifty miles an hour, killing the occupants instantly. Rachel and her sister, Rebecca (then seventeen, the raving beauty of the family), took months to recover from the initial shock. . . . and there were those who said that Rebecca never recovered at all. She had refused thereafter to ride in a horse-drawn vehicle—and later married a Mennonite at least partly (by her own admission) to escape the Amish proscription of automobiles. Rachel, too, had not ridden in a buggy on a highway until, four years later, Jacob Lapp had come courting.

Living then with her uncle, Elam Yoder, Rachel had suffered a long crisis of faith. She avoided attending services, questioning everything from the existence of God to the propriety of the Amish disdain for higher education. She had delayed her baptism until just before her marriage, yielding finally to Jacob's gentle urging. She had argued long and hard with Jacob about the wisdom of having children, citing the incidence of manic-depression and mental retardation among the Amish, attributed by some to the close intermingling of blood lines.

In this she was aided, abetted, and informed by her sister Rebecca, who was herself a manic-depressive, and who had committed herself, two years earlier, to the Mennonite-operated Brook Lane Hospital in Maryland. There she had met, fallen in love with, and married her psychiatrist—a devout Mennonite named Brand—and had never looked back to Lancaster County, except to correspond with Rachel.

And out of that correspondence had come the seeds —indeed the flowering—of Rachel's unrest. She had worried through her pregnancy with Samuel, and had refused herself to Jacob for three years thereafter, until it was possible to determine (after a visit by Rebecca and Dr. Brand) that Samuel was an entirely normal child. Then she had resumed a reasonably normal relationship with her husband, without telling him that she was taking birth control pills prescribed by Dr. Brand. After two or three more years, she was simply written off as barren by the community and her husband. And Rachel could not have cared less.

Yet she loved Jacob, and wanted to please him. And to please God. But she found herself constantly at odds, with this or that or something else. With a rule or a bishop or a bishop's wife. Seldom with Jacob. He, until the day he died, seemed to regard her as a natural, irreproachable wonder; as the most beautiful thing he had ever seen. She was beautiful; she knew that. She had grown into it almost reluctantly, because her beauty had only added to her problems. Her great gray-blue eyes, her perfectly boned face, her full lips, and lustrous brown hair—all were more of an embarrassment than an asset to an Amish wife. She covered them as best she could, just as she tried to cover her doubts. But there was no question—in her own mind, or in the minds of her Amish neighbors—that Rachel

15

Lapp, good and amiable though she certainly was, had some distance to go before she could be considered a proper and contented Amish woman.

And now that Jacob was dead and buried, she found herself more uneasy than ever. Rebecca was the only other survivor of her immediate family; and she—suddenly and almost desperately—wanted to see Rebecca. To sit down with her and discuss . . . everything. The world, the brevity of human life, the state of being Amish, God, Samuel's future, and the mysterious state of matrimony. She felt she needed urgently to talk, to get away, to gain some perspective on what she had been doing with the first thirty years of her life. And if that meant a trip to Baltimore, with Samuel in hand, then so be it. Whatever the doubts or the dangers, she felt she could do no other.

That night, after Daniel had gone home and Samuel had gone to bed, Rachel decided to speak to Eli. She waited until he had finished his nightly reading in the old German bible and had picked up *The Budget*. He rattled the newspaper loudly and glanced toward her just as she spoke.

"I think I will go to Baltimore."

Eli blinked at her. "You think what?"

"My sister in Baltimore? I want to visit her."

"You mean the Mennonite?"

"I mean Rebecca," Rachel said, somewhat sharply. "She married a Mennonite. But she still thinks of herself as Amish."

"And I," Eli said, drily, "I still sometimes think of myself as a young man."

"It is not the same thing. And she is my sister after all."

"But all the way to Baltimore? Alone?"

"I will take Samuel with me."

"This makes it better? An eleven-year-old boy?"

"I want him to meet his aunt."

"Let her come here."

16

"She has been sick. She should not travel."

"Nor should Samuel. He has never been out of Lancaster County."

"Neither have I," Rachel said, with not quite the emphasis she intended. Eli's eyes widened.

"So this is the purpose? To take a trip outside the county?"

Rachel sighed, strained to keep her tone even. "The purpose is to visit my sister." Then, after a moment: "It is also for me to get away."

Eli stared at her for a few seconds. "Get away? From what?"

Rachel eyed him steadily. "I think you know."

Eli spread his hands. "I do not, child. I do not."

"Then," Rachel said evenly, "since I must, I will tell you. But you certainly should have taken notice."

"Notice of what?" Eli said impatiently. "Speak of it. What is bothering you?"

"Daniel Hochleitner."

Eli stared at her pop-eyed. "Daniel? He has already spoken to you?"

"No," Rachel said. "Of course not. But he is always here. Just by his presence, he is pressing." She looked at Eli for a long moment. "I think you know this. I think you encourage it."

Again, Eli spread his hands. "What can I say, Rachel? Daniel is a fine young man. I encourage it—maybe since he would make you a fine husband. But he would never speak of it until there is a full year of mourning."

Rachel sighed heavily. "He would never speak of it, Eli. Not for a year. But by the end of the year he would have made himself so . . . so familiar, so much a member of the family, I would be in a corner to say yes."

"You don't like Daniel for a husband?"

"I don't like anybody for a husband, yet. I want to think about it for a long time. I want to get away."

Eli studied the top of her head as she stared down at the floor. "But we have work to do. We . . . we have

17

tobacco still for stripping, we have the milkhouse to paint, we have—"

"No!" Rachel said sharply, her head snapping up, her eyes shining. "We do not have work to do. The tobacco is all stemmed, the milkhouse does not need repainting, and there is three feet of snow on the ground. If it melts tomorrow, it will still be ten days before you can put horses in the field!"

"Child," Eli said.

"I am not a child, and do not continue to treat me as one. You are trying to *make* work, for us and for Daniel. And you are trying to push me into a corner. Well, I will not go into that corner. I will go to Baltimore."

She stood up, closed the lid on her sewing basket, reached to a shelf, put the sewing basket firmly in its place, and turned to the stove. She lifted the lids, picked up a bucket of coal, poured a covering of new coals on the fire, turned the damper to bank it for the night, put the lids back on, set the lid handle carefully to one side, and turned to face Eli.

"Rachel," he said, as soon as she turned to him. "I do not want this trip."

"Go to bed, Eli," Rachel said, walking to the door to the stairs. "God keep us this night."

CHAPTER THREE

By noon the next day, Eli had run out of arguments (he was primarily alarmed at the prospect of having to eat his own cooking), and Rachel was packed and ready to go. She had sent Samuel off to school with a note for his teacher about his impending absence, had written out a week of menus for Eli, and had gotten Elam Fisher, a Mennonite neighbor who had a telephone, to call Rebecca in Baltimore and tell her that she was on her way. All that remained was to get Eli to drive her to the railroad station in Lancaster, which she finally accomplished by threatening to walk.

All the way over to the schoolhouse to pick up Samuel, Eli lectured her about leaving so suddenly, leaving him in the lurch, and leaving without saying goodbye to Daniel Hochleitner. Daniel, as it happened, had gone in before dawn to the market in Lancaster and would, Eli assured her, be very upset at her abrupt departure. Rachel asked Eli to convey her apologies to Daniel, but went on to say that Daniel was not, after all, a member of the family and that she did not feel obliged to treat him as if he were.

They were by this time at the schoolhouse and Samuel was climbing into the buggy chattering excitedly about the trip and how he couldn't wait to get on the train. Presented with an as yet unventilated issue, Eli attacked at once.

"It's not right," he said to Rachel. "For a boy so young."

"Please, Eli," Rachel said tensely.

"Riding on a train. No good can come of it."

"Good can come of it," Rachel said. "It will get us to Baltimore."

"It is not our way, trains. Next you will be riding him around in a auto car."

"I will not. And what of those who go to Florida for the winter? They ride in autos. Or take the train."

"New Amish. Or Beachy."

"Some Old Order, too," Rachel insisted.

"Not in our district!"

Rachel sighed. "The point is our people do take trains when it is necessary."

"This is not necessary."

"It is more necessary than a vacation to Florida in the winter."

"And those who go to Florida are grown-up people. Not young boys to get corrupted."

"I won't get corrupted, grossdaddy," Samuel said. "I promise."

"You won't know it, Samuel," Eli said. "Corruption will come like a thief in the night and take your innocence from you—"

"Eli!" Rachel said sharply. "I am Samuel's mother. I will see to his innocence."

"How will you do this, riding him around on railroad trains?"

"I will do it!" Rachel snapped. "And that is the end of it!"

Eli looked at her somewhat startled. He opened his mouth to speak, then shut it again. It was Samuel who closed the discussion. He put a hand on Eli's near arm and spoke softly, "Don't worry, grossdaddy. I will keep a close walk with God. And with Mother."

* * *

They were in the waiting room when Daniel found them. Rachel saw him coming through the door and groaned inwardly. He was a tall, handsome man with flowing blond hair and a quick smile, and he had a fine sense of humor. But he was also a strict traditionalist, and the last thing Rachel needed that afternoon was another dose of tradition.

He came up smiling, looking from Rachel to Eli and back again. "I saw your horse outside. Is someone coming?"

"No," Eli said, snorting it out. "Rachel is going. And taking poor Samuel with her."

"I don't understand," Daniel said.

"Neither do I," Eli said.

"We're going to Baltimore to visit my sister," Rachel said. She got to her feet, glared at Eli, and took Daniel by the arm. "Come away," she said, leading him toward the ticket counter. "Eli won't listen."

"Don't you listen either, Daniel!" Eli called after them. "You talk good sense to her."

Daniel did very little talking. He attended her closely, his blue eyes solemn upon her, as she stated her case. "I haven't seen my sister, Rebecca, in more than five years," she said. "I want to see her again. Now."

Daniel nodded. "She cannot come here?"

"She came here last time. It is my turn," Rachel said. Then, hesitating, she added, "But that isn't the whole truth of it."

Daniel nodded. "You will tell me?"

Rachel sighed, looked away. "I need some time apart, Daniel. Some time to . . . to consider my options." She looked back at him. "You are part of that."

"I am glad to hear it," Daniel said. "But I did not presume. Or mean to presume."

"Of course you did," she said, fixing him coolly. "And I was flattered by it."

"Oh. I see."

"But I still need to get away."

"I understand, Rachel."

"I hope you do."

21

"No, I mean it. Go to your sister. Go with God."

Rachel looked at him for a long moment, then smiled. "Thank you, Daniel." She started to turn, then paused, touched his arm. "You are a good man. I am not looking to find another."

And, as she moved away, Daniel Hochleitner's grin was broad and beatific.

As the train rattled east through the low rolling hills and out of Lancaster County, Rachel sat staring out the window, thinking about the rest of her life. She had spoken somewhat bravely to Daniel of her options. And he had generously acted as if she had options. But the reality was that, as a young Amish widow, she had none. A young Amish widow was expected to remarry, sooner rather than later, but certainly within a year of her husband's death. She had some leeway, of course, as to which man she might choose, but she had to be brisk about it . . . and that was plainly that. There had to be a new man . . . a man to run the farm, a man to be a father to Samuel, a man to share her bed, a man to keep her pregnant. A man with whom to start all over again.

Rachel groaned. She didn't have any choice, yet she wanted a choice. She really didn't want to start all over again. Not yet, maybe not ever. She'd had her marriage, and it had had its moments. Even its days. But not its weeks, or its years. And she'd had her child, and was so well pleased with him that she had no desire to have another. Which was not the Amish way. Nothing Amish about it.

And that was what was bothering her most deeply. Was she ready to follow her sister out of the Amish faith? Was that why she was really going to see Rebecca? To seek aid and comfort? Had she already decided, subconsciously, to become a Mennonite? To leave the faith of her fathers and grandfathers? Mennonites were not doomed or damned, so to speak, but the Old Order Amish were the chosen. To leave was almost unthinkable. But was she, in fact, thinking it?

She prayed to God that it was not so. That it was merely a phase, a temptation. That it would not grow stronger as the train bore her farther and farther out of Lancaster County.

And when Samuel—who had been running up and down the aisle of the almost empty car, discovering marvels everywhere—came rushing back to tell her all about how the urinal in the men's room had a golden handle, Rachel hugged him to her and said, "Dearest Samuel, God keep you innocent."

PART ONE

CHAPTER FOUR

Rachel guided Samuel into the main room of the dingy 30th Street Station in Philadelphia, one hand in the small of his back. "Don't dawdle, Samuel," she said.

"They are all staring," Samuel said.

"They are all tourists," Rachel said. "Just like at home."

"Didn't they ever see Amish before?" Samuel said, somewhat disdainfully. Samuel, a very self-possessed young man, was very well aware that he looked different, that he *was* different, but it always surprised him that the English had to gawk. After all, he wasn't exactly a penguin.

"Don't let it bother you, Samuel."

Samuel looked up at his mother, the defiant tilt of her chin, and, as always, felt a surge of pride in being with her. "It doesn't bother me, Momma. It just wonders me."

"Come, come," Rachel said. "Here is the proper line."

They took their places in the line for the Baltimore train. People turned and stared, so Samuel immediately turned his back to them. And there, at the end of the adjoining line, was a pretty girl of his own age staring directly at him. A very pretty girl with twinkling eyes and a mischievous smile. Samuel smiled back at her, and she turned away and spoke softly to her mother. The mother looked around at Samuel, smiled a large, great-toothed smile, and said, quite loudly, "Oh, that's a little Amish boy! Isn't he cute?"

Samuel snapped around, set his face forward.

"What is it, Samuel?" Rachel asked.

"Just more English," Samuel said.

And then it was their turn at the window. Rachel showed the man her tickets. "We're going to Baltimore," she said. "Where is that train, please?"

"Delayed three hours," the man said. "You'll hear an announcement when it's time to board."

"Three hours? Why is that?"

"No idea, lady."

"But is this common?"

"Happens all the time. Just have a seat."

"Well, you might at least apologize," Rachel said, primly.

"Huh?" the man said, looking astonished. "Oh, yeah sure, lady. I'm sorry all to hell, right?"

Rachel turned, took Samuel's arm. "Stupid man," she said, and led Samuel over to one of the benches.

Rachel sat on the bench knitting somewhat furiously, the needles clicking sharply, her annoyance with the delay obvious to Samuel. "Are you angry, Momma?" he asked.

"Just a little, Samuel."

"Will you be all right?"

"I will be all right."

"Can I walk around a little, Momma?"

Rachel hesitated. "If you don't go so far. Try to stay where I can see you."

"Yes, Momma."

Samuel kissed his mother, turned and walked directly to the water fountain. He had a long drink, then walked past a bank of telephones where a whole line of

27

people were shouting into the black hand instruments. Samuel thought that if he were at the other end of these conversations, he would set the instrument aside until these people had stopped shouting.

He moved over to the escalators, and watched them for a time. He'd seen one before, in a hotel in Lancaster, but he hadn't been able to inspect it closely. Now he got right down, his hands to his knees, and looked at how the thing came out of the floor and went on up the hill. It looked to him very like a sileage conveyor, like the one that had killed his father. And this sudden thought bothered him so much that he backed away, thought to himself that he would never get on such a thing just to get up a flight of stairs. He backed into a pretty young woman who smiled and said, "Are you all right?"

"I am good," Samuel said.

"I'll bet you are," she said. "I could just wrap you up and take you home."

"No," Samuel said solemnly. "I don't do that."

The young woman laughed and moved away, leaving behind the aroma of gardenias.

Samuel walked on, looking back at his mother, making sure he kept her in sight. He came into a sort of gallery, another sitting room, and stopped short as he saw the angel.

It was a monstrous statuary, big as a horse. The angel was holding a dead soldier in its arms, and, as far as Samuel was concerned, it was clear that the angel was about to take the dead soldier up to heaven. But what does this mean? Samuel thought. Did this happen here? Did this soldier come home from a war to the Philadelphia railroad station, and die here, and get carried up to heaven by that angel? If so, what a fine thing for that angel to do, and what a fine thing for the people to see. And what a fine thing to have a statue to make people remember it.

He ran back to Rachel and told her all about it. Rachel took a look, from where she sat, at the angel, and said that Samuel might be right, but that it was probably meant to signify all of the war dead. "The English have a lot of war dead," she said. "And they put up such statues in their honor."

"Why do they have a lot?"

"Of statues?"

"Of war dead people?"

"Because they hold a lot of wars."

"Why don't they stop holding them?"

"I don't know, Samuel. I don't know."

An hour later, Samuel, who had fallen asleep on Rachel's shoulder, came awake and told his mother that he had to go to the toilet. He knew where it was; he had spotted it during his travels.

"You come right back," Rachel said.

"I will, Momma," Samuel said, starting away.

"Your hat," Rachel said. She put the hat on Samuel's head, kissed him. "Be careful," she said.

"Yes, Momma."

The men's room proved to be somewhat intimidating. There was a row of three trough-style urinals with water pouring down their backsides, all making a glugging noise that held Samuel at a distance. The troughs sat a bit too high for his purposes anyway, so Samuel turned to the stalls. He bent, holding his hat, to see if there was one unoccupied. They were, in fact, all unoccupied. Samuel was alone in the men's room. Samuel straightened, proceeded along the row of doors, selected the one next to last, entered, closed the door behind him. He unhooked his pants and relieved himself, thinking that the English certainly did not pay attention to their toilet houses the way they should, what with odd wads of paper and things here and there, and the smell of it all pretty bad, even by farm standards.

And he was finishing his business when he heard something out in the lavatory. He hooked himself up and went carefully to the door, and peeked out. There was a bearded young English in a big plaid jacket at the sinks. He seemed nervous, moved from one foot to the

29

other as he turned on the water, took it up in his hands, slopped it up against his face. He kept looking toward the door, as if he were expecting someone, but then— as Samuel heard someone else walk in, heavy-footed, *clump-clump*—the young English at the sink took one look, then turned back to the sink, took up some more water in his hands, washed his face again. Then there was the sound of footsteps going out, and, quickly the young English reached up behind a square tin that held the paper towels, felt around for a minute, then took out what looked like a small notebook. He flipped it open, glanced at it, then stuck one foot up on the sink, tucked the notebook into the top of his right boot, put his foot back down on the floor, and looked at himself in the mirror again.

Then more footsteps. A big black man entered and went to a sink at the far end of the room. Then another man came walking in quickly, came down to a sink just beyond where the other English stood, looked in the mirror, moved his jacket from one arm to the other, ran a comb through his hair. But then, suddenly, he snapped around, threw his jacket over the head of the young English and pulled him backwards and down to the floor. And, as he did this, the black man came running over with an open knife in his hand and used it to cut the young English's throat.

Samuel fell back, crouched down by the toilet in the rear of the cubicle. From there, trembling, he could see, beneath the door of the stall, the young English down on the floor, the jacket still over his head, the blood spurting from the gaping slash across his throat. Numbed by terror, frozen in his place of concealment by some primal instinct of survival, Samuel watched the young man's feet and arms flailing, and the pool of blood widening on the floor beneath his head. Samuel knew that he was dead. Like slaughtering a hog, he thought. They kick for a while, but they are dead once you cut the throat.

The black man turned to the sink, turned on the water, washed off the knife carefully, wiped it with a paper towel very carefully, then dropped it in the trash bin. Then he walked over to the dying man, stepped on his right foot to keep it from kicking, reached into the top of the dying man's boot, took out the notebook that the young English had taken from behind the towel dispenser. As he flipped through the notebook, he spoke to the other, who was still holding the jacket over the young English's head. "Get the fucker's watch."

"What?"

"I want his watch."

"Jesus," the other said.

"Get it!"

The other man let go of the young English's head. There was no further movement; he was dead for sure. The other man took the watch from the dead man's wrist, tossed it to the black man. The black man slipped it into his jacket pocket, then knelt on one knee by the dead man, put one finger to the right side of the young English's face.

"He's dead," said the other man.

"Just checking," said the black man.

"Let's get the fuck out of here."

"Don't rush me, hoss!" the black man snarled. "Don't you ever rush me!"

During this, Samuel had a full view of the black man's face. It was very black, with broad features—especially the nose—and eyes that looked almost feverish. At one moment he seemed to look right at Samuel, and Samuel got down behind the commode and held his hands over his eyes.

"What the hell are you waiting for?" the other man said.

"Just want to make sure we're alone," the black man said.

Samuel looked around to see the black man taking a large revolver out of a shoulder holster, getting to his feet. Samuel ducked now, watched the black man walk to the first toilet stall at the far end. He heard him snatch open the stall door, slam it shut, then saw him move down to the next one. Samuel forced himself to his feet, went to the door of his stall, tried to lock it. The latch stuck, wouldn't push through the hasp. Samuel's hands began to tremble, and he began to hit at the latch. The door of the stall next to his was banged open, and in that instant the latch went into place. Samuel fell back to the rear of the stall, crouched down by the toilet. He could see the black man's feet outside, and jumped as there was a smash against the stall door. The latch held. The black man backed away, one foot left the floor, and a powerful kick hit the stall door. The latch still held.

"Goddamn," the black man said, "This one's locked." Samuel saw him back away again, for another kick, and Samuel did the only thing left to him. He ducked under the partition into the adjoining stall—the one the black man had just checked. He brushed his hat off on the bottom of the partition, reached back, and snatched the hat back out of sight just as the black man's foot hit the stall door. It flew open, the latch rattling on the floor as it came free of its moorings.

"Will you for Christ's sake come on!" the other man shouted from out near the door.

"Coming, man." The black man's legs fairly whipped along as he turned and headed out. "What the fuck you so nervous about?" he said. "Thing went down like a whore in a gold mine."

And they were gone.

Samuel eased out of the stall very slowly, eyes averted from the body of the dead man. Until the last instant, when he had to step past the dead man's head, had to look down to avoid stepping in the pool of blood. And saw the dead man's eyes. And he knew the man was dead, because his eyes looked exactly like those of a dead hog.

CHAPTER FIVE

Zenovich!" John Book said, slamming the car into a long, tire-squealing curve that brought them broadside into Penn Square, "How the hell'd they get onto Zenovich?"

Elton Carter, Book's partner—a slight, wiry man with wearily amused eyes—ignored what he assumed was a rhetorical question. It wasn't.

"Well?" Book demanded.

Carter glanced at him, taking in for the ten thousandth time the powerfully built frame behind the wheel. Not overwhelming for size, perhaps, but for raw intensity and unyielding willpower, John Book was a case to be reckoned with. And that latent fury, which was something Carter never really understood and never, *ever* tampered with, was never far below the surface. It gave Book an edge, all right. Funnily enough, Carter thought, there were times—even at thirty-four—when Book looked relatively harmless; his wide, open features could take on a boyish charm, and he invariably looked like he was a day or so late getting to the cleaners.

This, however, was not one of those times.

Carter sighed, pointing out patiently, "You bring

him in from Atlantic City like you did, they're going to see him coming from Mays Landing north. I mean, they know from Atlantic City."

"Bullshit," Book said. "He wasn't on the police force down there six months when I recruited him."

Carter shrugged. "Six months is long enough."

"So, if they got Zenovich, the whole operation is in trouble. Because he was a shrewd kid, knew the drill, and stuck to it."

"I'd say the whole operation is down the fucking tubes," Carter said.

"Why would you say that? I've spent ten goddamned months on this thing!"

"I'd say that because what Zenovich was picking up tonight was the book on all of the street contacts."

"No, he wasn't."

"Yes, he was. Street contacts, along with the police officers doing the banking for each one of them. And we're talking names, addresses, phone numbers of the contacts and the officers."

"Jesus Christ! I didn't think that would be ready for a month! Two months!"

"Like you said," Carter said drily. "Zenovich was one hell of an investigator."

"Why didn't I know about this?"

"I would have told you, Johnny. But I only found out myself, from Zenovich, four hours ago." He looked at his watch. "Five hours and five minutes ago. He tried to get you, but they said you were taking a steam bath."

"I was! Jesus pistolled Christ! No wonder they hit him!" Book put the wheel hard over, missed bashing the back of a bus by a few inches, and came in against the curb in front of the 30th Street Station with a thump that almost turned the car over on its side.

"Good job, Book," Carter said sarcastically. "For a minute there, I thought we'd arrive in a routine manner, without damage to the vehicle."

John Book, with Carter right flank rear, blew through the milling mob in front of the station with one

34

hand—thrust out palm first in front of him—saying, "No comment, friends," to the minicam crews, newsmen and women, and photographers who had gathered on the sidewalk. As they cleared the doors into the station, Book glanced back at Carter and snapped, "How the hell did they find out so fast? How come I'm always the last one to know?"

"Your own fucking fault," Carter said. "You take fucking baths, you get the dirty fucking news last, right?"

"Right," Book said. "And up yours."

"And up yours, too, commander," Carter said.

The uniforms, controlling the crowd, scowled as Book and Carter came through. Book was used to it. The uniforms—indeed, all cops anywhere—hated the cops who policed other cops. Book had chosen the job happily. Cops everywhere, but especially in Philadelphia, needed policing, and Book had taken up the challenge and opprobrium of it because it suited him to hold his peers to their given standards. For another thing, he hated hypocrites, and was not at all uncomfortable with the role of keeper of organizational honor. But it was the intensity at which he went at his job that both surprised and further alienated his colleagues, particularly the ones who had something to hide.

Book was drawn to policework in the beginning much because of the mental picture he formed of his father, growing up in the small frame house behind the Convent of the Sacred Heart, a few blocks from the turgid, brown currents of the Delaware River. A mental picture was all he had—apart from a few stiffly posed black and white snapshots among his mother's mementos—because his father died when John was five. Frank Book, commercial cabinetmaker by trade, was killed when he walked into a liquor store for a sixpack of Rheingold and discovered a robbery in progress. Impulsively trying to intervene, he was shot to death on the sidewalk for his pains.

This possibly ill-advised moment of valor had a

calamitous impact on the lives of the surviving Books. Beyond depriving John and his seven-year-old sister, Elaine, of a father, the incident made a splash in the press, with photographs and front-page headlines. Frank Book was hailed as a hero, and the public relations department of the police department seized an opportunity to hype the public's responsibility to enlist in the War Against Crime, whatever the cost. John Book saw his own picture in the *Inquirer,* decked out in a miniature police uniform presented to him by the Police Benevolent League. The Commissioner appeared on the front porch one morning with an entourage of newspapermen and a proclamation signed by the Mayor. And Mary Book was permanently inducted into the Philadelphia Police Auxiliary. Mary Book, a shy, impressionable woman, more than a little dazed by all the sudden notoriety, attended auxiliary meetings for the rest of her days with a pious regularity usually reserved for religious devotions. In addition to occupying her Tuesday nights, Mary Book thus assured her young son of continuous contact with various policemen, policemen's wives and policemen's sons and daughters for the remainder of his childhood.

All of this created a certain amount of confusion in the boy, and it took John Book some years to sort out exactly what kind of man his father really had been. Over a period of time he discovered that, while Frank Book was no epic hero, he was indeed a very decent man—quiet, with few friends, who had abandoned an independent carpentry business for the job security of factory furniture building. Still, he had moonlighted in a small woodshop he built over the family garage, which Mary Book, after his death, kept locked as though it were a shrine.

Venturing into the woodshop late one afternoon in his ninth year, having filched the key from his mother's jewelry box, John Book for the first time began to understand his father. Allowing his eyes to travel slowly over the dusty, cobwebbed awls and planes and other tools neatly arranged in their racks, the glues long hardened in their containers, the small cans of paint with faded labels, the half-finished sideboard standing upright in the middle of the floor, the boy began to understand that his father had lived and breathed and worked well with his hands in this place, that these tools responded to his touch, and that his craft would have brought to completion the handsome piece of furniture under his hands.

And with that understanding, for the first time, came a profound sense of loss, and the realization that Frank Book's death—while certainly a momentary triumph of personal heroism—was equally a gross injustice. John Book's father, when all was said and done, was a victim.

This realization on the part of the boy, which hardened over time into an underlying anger, more than any of the rest of it set him on the path of a career as a cop.

As John Book saw it, his father had been a good guy and that wasn't enough. But a cop was a good guy who could kick ass. And John Book, Lord knows, dearly loved to kick ass.

Zenovich lay where he had fallen, the puddle of blood blackening under his head. Lab technicians and police photographers were at work, and there was the usual stir of slight confusion. Book moved at once to take charge, looking around at the plainclothesmen, barking, "Who's first shirt here?"

"I am."

Book looked to a man named Walker from homicide. "What's your reading?"

Walker squinted at him. "He one of yours?"

"He was."

"Cut his throat. Found the knife in the garbage. Wiped clean. Professional job. Still got his wallet and his piece. Wasn't no robbery."

"One-man job?"

"Two, more like."

"Who found him?"

"A Amish kid."

"What?"

"I wouldn't lie to you. Ask him," Walker said, indicating an ancient black man who was standing to one side, looking mostly at the ceiling.

Book went over to him. "Who found the body?"

"Oh no, daddy. I didn't find no body. I merely gave out word of the findin'. Big fuckin' difference, daddy."

"I didn't say you found it," Book said, sighing.

"I mean, I am merely the fuckin' maintenance, daddy."

"Who found the body, and cut the shit!"

"Out there," the old man said, pointing through the door into the waiting room. "See? The kid in the funny black threads? He found him."

Book looked out, saw Samuel and Rachel sitting against one another in one corner of the bench. And he thought: The Lord moves in mysterious ways. And who the hell am I to argue?

Book bent slowly to Samuel, spoke softly, "Hello, there."

Samuel looked at Book, then turned to his mother. "Momma?"

"What do you want of my son?" Rachel said.

Book blinked as he took his first look at her. Just what I needed, he thought. A beautiful woman in black. "I'm a police officer," he said, showing her his badge. "I'm going to have to talk to the boy. What's his name?"

"My name's Samuel," Samuel said. "Samuel Lapp."

"But what happened here is none of his affair," Rachel said. "We're on our way to Baltimore. My sister is expecting us. Our train is leaving soon."

"There'll be another train," Book snapped, and instantly regretted his short tone. For one thing, he needed her cooperation. And for another, with her porcelain complexion untarnished by makeup, and her clear, round blue eyes confronting him directly, she *was* indeed a remarkably beautiful woman. In fact, he thought on reflection, the simple, dark dress only set off that fresh, unworldly beauty. Purity was the notion that sprang into Book's mind; a mind decidedly unaccustomed to the use of that word.

He modified his tone, and, speaking to both of them, said "Listen, the man who was killed tonight was a police officer." He looked to Samuel. "It's my job to find out who did it, Sam. Can you help me?"

"I don't know," Samuel said, stammering a bit. "But I saw him."

Book frowned. "You saw the man who was killed, you mean?"

"No, I saw the man who killed the other."

"You saw him?" Book, squatting in front of Samuel now, turned, looked up to Carter. "Anybody know about this?"

"*I* didn't know about it, so I doubt it."

"Right," Book said, turning back to Samuel. "Now, Sam, when you say you saw him, the man who killed Zenovich—I mean, the other man—tell me just *when* did you see him? As he was leaving the men's room?"

"Yes," Samuel said. "And before that."

"Before that?"

"Yes."

"Would you tell me about it, Sam? From the beginning?"

"I went to the room, and I went into one of the little places." Samuel looked to Rachel.

"You went into one of the cubicles?"

Samuel spoke quickly in the dialect to Rachel, and Rachel translated. "One of the stalls," she said.

"Right," Book said. "And?"

"And the young English came in, then another came in and put his jacket over the young English's face, and then the other man came with the knife. And cut his throat open like a pig."

Book stared for an instant—the matter-of-fact manner of the report stunned him. He glanced around at Carter, then returned to Samuel. "Did you see these men? Their faces?"

"I saw the one with the knife?"

"And what did he look like?"

"He was . . . he was," Samuel stammered. He started to turn to Rachel, then pointed at Carter. "He was like him."

"He means black," Carter said.

"Do you mean black?"

Now Samuel did confer with his mother, and Rachel nodded. "Black," she said.

"But not *schtumpig*," Samuel said to his mother.

"Not what?" Book said.

"Not *schtumpig*," Rachel said. She leaned to Book, attempting to save Carter's feelings. "On the farm, a pig born small in the litter is *schtumpig*. A runt."

"Right," Book said. "He wasn't a runt."

"I got the message," Carter said, good-naturedly. "He was a big man, right, Sam?"

"Yes. Big and black."

Book turned to look at Carter. "That limits it a little," Book said.

"Sure does," Carter said. "One third of South Philly."

"Would you recognize him if you saw him again, Sam? Or saw his picture?"

"Yes," Samuel said.

"Book!" barked a man, his voice like something out of an asphalt tuba. "I want to talk to you!"

Book turned, nodded. "Be right with you, Terry."

"Now, Captain!"

"Be right back, Sam, Mrs. Lapp," Book said.

The intruder was Captain Terry Donahue, Chief of Homicide, a big, bluff bull of a man with a cigar sticking out of his face like a lance. He looked at Book down the length of the cigar, and said, "This Zenovich was your man?"

"Right."

"I'm sorry, John. But it's still homicide's case."

"I want it, Terry."

"What have you got?"

"An eyewitness."

40

"That and fifty cents will sometimes get you a short bus ride."

"I want to work it."

Donahue eyed Book, hesitated, then nodded. "You got it, John."

"Appreciate it."

"You know, John, you ought to think about coming back to homicide. You stick with Internal Affairs, you won't have a friend left in the world."

Book smiled, nodded. "So I'll buy a dog."

Donahue regarded him coldly. "There was something about you I used to like, Johnny. What the hell was it?"

Book looked back at him with a hard, baleful eye. "I don't know, Donahue. I guess I just used to be different. I guess I used to be an asshole, just like you."

Donahue smiled. "You were running Zenovich, and he got snuffed. If I was you, John boy, I'd watch my ass."

"I will watch your ass, Donahue," Book said softly. "And if it gets in my way, I'll cut it off and feed it to you."

Donahue took the cigar out of his mouth, spat the tip on the floor. "Schaeffer's outside, wants to see you. And the next time you see my ass, you can kiss it." Donahue turned, walked away.

"Stay with them," Book said to Carter. "Keep them right here."

"Right, Captain," Carter said. "My regards to the commodore."

Deputy Chief Paul Schaeffer smiled and waved as Book came out of the station. Book thought, So far, so good. He walked around to the driver's side of the big Mercury sedan, opened the door, spoke to the driver. "Go get a cup of coffee, Stan."

The driver, a uniformed cop, looked to Schaeffer. "Bring me one. Black. No hurry."

The driver got out, and Book eased in under the

steering wheel, looked to Schaeffer. "You didn't have to make a personal appearance, Paul."

"A cop down, I show up. How are you, Johnny?"

"I've been far better."

"I understand. And I understand you've got an eyewitness."

"An Amish boy."

"I heard. How positive is he?"

"Couldn't be more so. He saw the entire murder."

"What's it all about?"

"They were after a drop, and they got it. A list of names Zenovich was about to deliver. Street chemists. The guys processing P2P into speed."

"P2P again."

"Very popular stuff."

"And there's a link to the department?"

"I wouldn't be here if there wasn't."

"Well, I hope you can develop it real fast, one way or the other. I mean the press . . . well, you know the press. We're the speed capital of the country. The Commissioner is getting exercised."

"The Commissioner could use some exercise."

Schaeffer, a man with a kindly, avuncular face, chuckled. "You're my boy, Johnny. Go get 'em."

"Right," Book said, "but do me a favor?"

"Name it."

"Keep Terry Donahue and homicide off my back."

"You got it."

"Thanks, Paul."

"But you've also got something else, Johnny."

"What's that?"

"A deadline. When word gets to the newspapers that Zenovich was a cop, they'll set up the bagpipes. You got twenty-four hours, Johnny. After that, I've got to give the case, and the witness, to homicide."

"You couldn't make it forty-eight?"

"I couldn't."

"I'll make it work, Paul. My regards to Marilyn."

"Thanks, Johnny, I'll tell her." As Book started to slide out, Schaeffer touched his arm. "Tell you what.

Why don't you and that blonde—what's her name?—why don't you come over for dinner Sunday?"

"What's-her-name moved to Buffalo."

"Oh. Well, stay in touch, Johnny. Remember, twenty-four hours."

"Keep a stiff one, Paul," Book said, slamming the door. And he walked away thinking, He's in on it, folks. I can smell it all over him.

CHAPTER SIX

S amuel stared with fascination out the car window as it cruised along 13th Street. This was a wretched corridor of slums, vermin-ridden eateries, porno shops, storefront missions, and the faces of the ambulatory poor and desperate. Mostly the faces . . .

These ragged, ravaged men and women represented infinite mystery to the boy; their coming and going amid the squalor. Surely there must be a purpose to it, if only he could puzzle it out. Because in Samuel's Amish world there was usually serious purpose behind every action. That the denizens of these rank alleyways and filthy gutters were stripped of purpose—serious or otherwise—by poverty, prejudice, inner-city angst or whatever, was worlds beyond his comprehension.

His mother was not beset by such musings, although it was all she could do to shut the passing city-scape out of her mind, and fight back the terrifying feeling that events were cartwheeling completely out of control.

"Where are you taking us?" she demanded apprehensively from the back seat.

Book glanced back at her. He was driving, with Carter beside him. He hadn't explained what he was about, and really didn't want to. But her wide challenging eyes changed his mind.

"We're going to a suspect," he said. "I want Sam to look at him."

"You have no right to do this thing."

"Yes, I do," Book said grimly. "Your son is a material witness to a homicide."

The strain in Rachel's voice increased. "You don't understand. We have nothing to do with your laws."

"Doesn't surprise me," Book said, glancing at Carter. "We meet a lot of people like that."

"It is not for jokes."

"Right. No joke. Listen, I know a little about the Amish—"

Rachel gave him a sharp, challenging look. "How little?"

Book bit back his exasperation. "I meant I know something—Jesus—I mean look, *everybody* in Pennsylvania knows *something* about you people . . . horses, mules, carriages, no electricity—"

Rachel broke in with a clipped tone. "I agree. You do know a *little.*"

Book boiled for a moment, then turned to her with dogged determination. "What I was trying to say, Mrs. Lapp, is that I know this whole thing has to be an ordeal for you, and I'm really sorry you and Sam got involved."

Rachel kept her eyes riveted straight ahead. "You are not sorry."

"I'm not?"

"No, you're glad. Because now you've got a witness."

"Is that right?" He shifted uncomfortably behind the wheel.

"Yes. And I heard the other police talking about you."

"What did they have to say?" Book inquired, knowing he probably wasn't going to like the answer.

"They don't like you very much."

45

Book glanced at Carter, who just shook his head. "Well," Book said, "they kid a lot."

"They were not kidding," Rachel said. She looked at him. "I think I would be careful, if I were you."

Samuel leaned to his mother, spoke to her in the dialect. Book glanced back. "What'd he say?"

"He wants to know your name," Rachel said. "I told him we don't need to know anything about you."

Book looked around at Samuel. "My name is Book, Sam. John Book."

"And *his* name," Rachel said, "is Samuel. Not Sam."

"Yes, ma'am," Book said, raising his eyebrows at Carter. "But you can call me John."

"Hey, Sammy!" Book shouted out the car window at a man who had just darted from a doorway. "Get your skinny ass over here!"

The man paused. "That you, Book?"

"That's me, Book," Book said. "Got ten iron men for you."

Sammy trotted over to the car. "Ten?"

"You tell me what I want to know."

"Try me."

"Where's Coalmine?"

Sammy was looking into the back seat. "What the hell you got there, the Salvation Army?"

"Coalmine, Sammy."

"Try Happy Valley. Where's my ten."

"Right here, Sammy. Keep the faith." Book handed the man the ten dollar bill, drove off, spoke to Carter. "Happy Valley? New turf for Coalmine."

"He needs new turf," Carter said. "About six feet deep of it."

Book, having gone by the Happy Valley bar, socked the car into reverse and backed up, came to shuddering stop in front of it.

"Thank you, Mr. Book!" Rachel said from the back

seat. "Thank you for snapping my head around on my neck again! Thank you very much!"

"Sorry about that," Book said.

"I only wish I could make you sorrier!" Rachel said. "Because if I could I certainly would!"

"Yes, ma'am," Book said. "Now, if you'll excuse us, we have to go in here and look for a dude, who we—"

"Look for a what?"

"A man. And we will lock you inside the car while we are gone, for your safety."

"You will not lock us in!"

Book sighed. "Okay, lady, I will not lock you in." He glanced at Carter. "The poor bastard who gets into this car will wish to Christ he hadn't, anyway," he said softly.

"What did you say?" Rachel said.

"I said you are such a charming lady no harm can possibly come to you," Book said.

Book and Carter climbed out of the car, went quickly inside.

The Happy Valley bar was dark, smoke-filled, packed to the walls, and almost exclusively black. Book saw two other white faces, and both of those behind the bar.

"You lookin' for a good time, honey?" said a strikingly pretty girl at the bar.

"Not tonight, momma," Book said.

"Looking for Coalmine," Carter said.

"Oh, oh," the girl said. "He down back, at the cigarettes machine."

The man called Coalmine was standing with his back to the bar, opening a package of cigarettes—a big, burly man, impeccably dressed. He had to have noticed the near silence that had fallen over the bar upon the entrance of the two policemen, but he gave no sign. Book turned to Carter, muttered, "Cover me."

Carter nodded, put his right hand to his shoulder holster. "You covered, White-eyes."

Book moved very quickly, closed to an arm's length of Coalmine before he spoke. "You like a breath of fresh air, Coalmine?"

"Fuck off," Coalmine said, not turning around.

"I need you outside, asshole."

"What you need, cop, I'll give you, you keep pushin'."

Book struck with practiced speed. He kicked Coalmine behind his right knee, and, as the big man went into a falling half-turn, he locked his left arm around his head in a choke hold, punched him twice in the eyes with his right hand, and walked him toward the door, calling out, "Clear the goddamned way, people!" He rammed Coalmine through the crowd, Carter doing what he could to move bodies to either side, and they came out onto the sidewalk at a near trot. Carter immediately turned and covered Book's flank, as Book pulled Coalmine over toward the car. "Never mind that!" Book said to Carter. "Lower the back window!"

"Right!" Carter said, and rushed to the car.

"What is this?" Rachel said, as Carter pulled the door open, started to work the window down.

"Just a little I.D. session," Carter said. He finished with the window, slammed the door as Book, wrestling a bit now with Coalmine, thumped the big man in the forehead with the heel of his right hand, then wheeled him in a half circle and slammed him hard across the hood of the car.

"You going to behave yourself?" Book shouted. "Or do I got to lean on you?" Coalmine, most of his wind knocked out on the hood, grunted. "Okay then, come here!" Book heaved him up to his feet, hauled him down the side of the car to the rear window, thrust Coalmine's head in through it. "Sam! Take a look! Take a good look! Is this the man you saw?"

"I can't see," Samuel said.

"Put some light on him!" Book shouted to Carter. Carter found the flashlight in the front seat, shined it into Coalmine's face. "This the man, Sam?"

Samuel, being held closely by Rachel, looked into Coalmine's staring, blood-rimmed eyes. "No," Samuel said.

"What'd he say?" Book shouted.

"He said no!" Rachel shouted right back. "Now go away!"

"You sure, Sam?"

"Yes," Samuel said.

"He's sure, John Book! Now you get away from us!" Rachel said, close to tears.

Book pulled Coalmine back, released him, shoved him away. "Honest mistake," Book said.

Other men had come crowding out of the Happy Valley, and backed Coalmine as he growled at Book, "You fuckin' cops think you can come in here and do us any way you want. One of these nights, we gonna do *you!*"

Carter brought out his pistol as the men surged forward. "No fools here tonight! Don't show me no fools!"

"Tell you what, Coalmine. Anytime you're ready, you let me know, I'll come down here alone," Book said. "You didn't maybe do this murder, but you've done your share. And I mean to have your ass."

"I'll let you know," Coalmine said. "I'll let you know about two minutes before I hand you your fuckin' head!"

There was a small cheer from the gathered men. Book grinned, nodded to Carter. "All back to normal," he said. "Let's roll."

Carter climbed in as Book eased behind the wheel. "Back to normal, my ass," he growled. "Come within an inch of getting wiped."

"No way," Book said. "Nice respectful citizens, every one."

"John Book!" said Rachel from the back seat, trying to keep the terror that had surged within her breast out of her voice, "You listen to me! I will have no further part in this, nor will my son! As God stands between us!"

"Well," Book said, "we do have one more suspect we'd like to check—"

"Absolutely not!" Rachel shrilled. "I will not have it, I will not allow it!"

Book sighed; the woman's tone was indeed in the ragged-edge range. "Okay," he said. "That's it for tonight."

"That's enough forever!" Rachel cried. "We want to go to bed!"

Book cocked his head at Carter inquiringly. His partner nodded. "If you're asking me, the lady's got my vote."

"You take us to a place we can sleep," Rachel said stridently. "My son is exhausted, thanks to you!"

"How about the Bellevue Stratford?" Book said. "Understand it's four-star."

"We will not go to a hotel," Rachel said in a firm voice. "We do not stay at hotels."

"Right." Book nodded at this latest revelation. He glanced at Carter, who shrugged helplessly. Then the solution to the problem came to him. He nodded, "Just happens that I've got a good four-star alternative in mind."

CHAPTER SEVEN

Elaine, Book's sister, snatched the door open and glared out, hostile-eyed. "Well, for Christ's sake," she said, looking at Rachel and Samuel, "you didn't say they were refugees!" She eyed Book malevolently. "You inconsiderate bastard," she said, "I told you I had company."

"It's an emergency," Book said. "These people are Amish. They don't stay in hotels."

"Amish? Well, why the hell didn't you say so?" Elaine spoke to Rachel. "Come in, honey. I didn't mean to be rude."

Rachel ushered Samuel in reluctantly, walked past Elaine, smiling a very small smile. She looked through a door, saw a kitchen piled with dirty dishes and empty beer cans, closed her eyes, moved on.

Book pulled Elaine to one side, whispered through his teeth. "What the hell do you mean, company? Aren't the boys here?"

"They're upstairs, asleep."

"You've got a man here, and the kids are upstairs asleep?"

"Don't give me any of your moralistic shit, John, or

I'll toss you out on your ass!" Elaine said, also hissing through her teeth. "And, anyway, the kids like Fred."

"Oh, Fred," Book said, rolling his eyes. "Good old Fred."

Elaine showed Rachel and Samuel to the spare bedroom, and Samuel tumbled into one of the twin beds and fell sound asleep with no urging whatever. Rachel donned her nightgown, knelt to say her prayers —thanking God, first, that they hadn't lost their baggage in all of the confusion—and was just asking God to deliver her and Samuel from John Book when there came a knock at the door.

She opened to Elaine, who looked just as disheveled and disoriented as she had earlier.

"Listen," Elaine said, "I'm sorry to bother you. Is everything okay?"

"Everything's fine," Rachel said.

"I . . . I like your nightgown."

"You're kind to say so."

"John tells me you're Amish."

"That's right."

"Well, you're welcome here."

"Thank you."

"Goodnight," Elaine said, somewhat awkwardly.

"Goodnight," Rachel said, as Elaine closed the door behind her.

Samuel woke up as soon as the door was closed. "Momma?"

"Yes, dear."

"I don't want to stay here."

"It's all right, darling," Rachel said, going to him.

"They are not good people."

Rachel frowned. "They are English. They do the best they can."

But she was thinking about the dirty kitchen and the man upstairs in the woman's bed. For a moment she felt an intense longing for her own immaculate kitchen and the familiar order of Eli's good farm. Samuel seemed to sense her uncertainty.

"It's all right, Momma," Samuel said, and he was asleep again almost as soon as his eyes closed.

Rachel woke suddenly, looked over to Samuel's bed, saw that he was gone. She got up at once, dressed, went out into the hallway. As soon as she heard the sound of the television set, she went toward it, telling herself that it had better not be.

But it was. There was Samuel sitting on the living room floor, between Timmy and Buck—Elaine's children—eating cereal out of a box and watching an animated cartoon on the television.

"Samuel!" Rachel said sharply, but he didn't appear to have heard her. "Samuel, do you hear me?" No reaction from Samuel. Rachel walked briskly over and pulled the television plug from the wall.

Elaine woke up an hour later with a throbbing headache. The sight of Fred's hairy back rising and falling next to her drove her to her feet. She went into the bathroom, took three aspirin tablets, looked at herself in the mirror, groaned, told herself that she had houseguests and must prepare them some breakfast. She groaned again, thinking about what the kitchen must look like.

She went out into the living room, and stopped short, unable, for a moment, to accept the evidence of her eyes. There was her older son, Timmy, pushing a carpet sweeper back and forth across the living room rug. And there was her younger son, Buck, diligently wiping at the furniture with a clothful of lemon oil. Beyond them, the Amish boy was polishing the big front window. None of them noticed Elaine's presence, and she decided at once to let it go unannounced. She had no intention of interrupting such extraordinary industry.

She moved quietly on into the kitchen, and stopped short again. It fairly sparkled, and there was the Amish woman at the far end vigorously mopping the floor. Elaine stared for a moment, then opened her mouth to speak. But, just as she did so, the Amish woman turned, smiled at her, and said, "Good morning, Elaine."

"Good morning," Elaine said. "My God . . . Rachel, is it?"

"Rachel."

"Rachel, you didn't have to do all this."

"I wanted to. You were very kind to take us in last night. I put water on for coffee."

"Oh, good . . . good." She almost said "Good Amish woman," but caught herself. She sat down at the kitchen table. "Very nice of you, Rachel."

"Not at all. I needed something to do. I was so angry with your brother. He is so . . . so *glotzkopp!*"

"*Glotzkopp?* Yeah, that sounds like John all right."

"I told him we could not break in on you in the middle of the night that way. But he would not listen."

"*Glotzkopp.* I like that."

"It means—"

"Don't tell me what it means," Elaine said, waving one hand. "It's better I don't know. I wouldn't want to give him the satisfaction."

"The satisfaction?"

"Of telling him what it means."

"Oh," Rachel said. "You are not fond of him, either?"

"I can't stand him," Elaine said. "From his *glotz* to his *kopp*. And his goddamned gun. Excuse me," she said, shrugging. "How's the coffee coming?"

"Good," Rachel said. "In a minute."

"Tell me something," Elaine said. "You aren't carrying a gun or a club. How'd you manage to put my kids to work?"

"Oh," Rachel said. "I made it a contest. The one who does best gets his cereal back first." Rachel went back to her mopping. "Children like to help. They only need to be kept after a little bit."

"Is that right?" Elaine said coldly. She realized the Amish woman meant no harm, but there was something in the way Rachel spoke that struck Elaine, in her present ragged state, as insufferably complacent. She knew she had a quick temper, and told herself now to hold it, but the sight of this woman mopping her floor and dispensing advice was simply too much. "Listen, lady," Elaine said. "No offense, but I figure I know as much about kids as you do, having had two of the same! And I'm not sure I like your coming in here, handing out homey wisdom and turning my goddamned house upside down!"

Rachel's smile faded. She stopped mopping, stared at Elaine. "But I only wanted to help."

Elaine stood up, snatched the mop out of Rachel's hands, began to mop furiously. "So you helped! Good for goody-two-shoes! Listen, maybe I'm not a world-class *hausfrau,* and maybe I don't have time to polish the goddamned china and keep after the goddamned kids!" She paused to glare at Rachel. "But I do the best I can! It's none of your business, but I don't happen to have a full-time man around the house to support me! So I sell cosmetics in a goddamned drugstore, and sometimes I can even pay the rent on time!" She took a particularly angry swipe with the mop, knocked over a waste basket, then hurled the mop clattering across the floor. She put her hands to her hips, glared at Rachel. "So maybe I'm not Mary goddamned Poppins, but maybe I don't need to have it jammed down my goddamned throat, either!"

Rachel was almost speechless. "I am very sorry," she managed. "I had no idea. . . ."

"Jesus Christ," Fred said from the doorway. "What the hell happened?" He stood, in a bathrobe, surveying the immaculate kitchen. "Somebody die, Elaine, and leave you a broom?"

"You son of a bitch!" Elaine shouted. "Get out of my way!"

And Elaine pushed past Fred and strode out of the kitchen. Fred looked after her, blinked around at Rachel. "What got into her?" he said.

"Oh," Rachel said, "I didn't get her coffee ready in time."

* * *

"I brought you some coffee," Rachel said.

Elaine lay across her rumpled bed, sobbing into her pillow. Rachel closed the door behind her, then took a seat by the bed, placing the cup of coffee on the edge of a nightstand next to an ashtray overflowing with cigarette butts. "Just put it down," Elaine said.

"I also want to apologize," Rachel said. "I didn't mean to hurt you."

Elaine looked up, her eyes red and swollen, and said, "It's okay. Maybe I needed hurting." She pulled herself up into a sitting position, wrapping her arms around the pillow and shaking her head and sighing. "Look, I shouldn't have blown my stack like that. It's like, somehow, I seem to have let everything slip, get away from me." She glanced at Rachel helplessly. "And you sort of made me face it."

"You did the same for me," Rachel said, smiling, almost giggling.

"What? What are you giggling at?"

"Fred," Rachel said, one hand to her mouth. "The way you screamed at him."

"Oh God," Elaine said. "Fred."

"At home, you'd never hear a woman scream at a man like that."

Elaine cocked her head, picked up the coffee cup, and took a sip. "No? Why not?"

Rachel shrugged. "You just wouldn't. It is not the Amish way." She shook her head, but then stopped, set her jaw. "But I tell you, I think it would have done me good if I could have screamed at your brother last night."

Elaine suddenly looked at Rachel with new interest. What the hell was this? she thought. This here Amish lady is a little hung up on my brother John. "Aren't you married?" Elaine said bluntly.

Rachel's eyes widened, and she looked away. "My husband was killed," she said. "In a farm accident."

"I'm sorry. How long ago was that?"

"Two months. A little less."

Elaine nodded. "Well, listen, that's none of my business, really. And I don't know how you got mixed up with my brother, John. But don't you let that self-righteous son of a bitch push you around. Okay?"

Rachel looked at Elaine closely, then smiled as though they were sharing a secret. "Okay," Rachel said. "I will not."

CHAPTER EIGHT

Book arrived at Elaine's door a few minutes after eight o'clock, feeling as if he'd been dragged all night behind a horse. He hadn't slept, having been out all night with Carter, running down leads and notions. All of it to no purpose. He accepted a cup of coffee from Elaine—who looked somehow amused by him— and got the Amish woman and her son out of the house and into his car as soon as he gracefully could.

On the way downtown, Rachel kept looking at him out of the corner of her eye, and Book finally turned and made inquiry. "I got rhubarb growing out of my right ear, or something?"

"I don't think so."

"Then what's your problem? Why are you eyeing me?"

"My problem is that I don't think my son and I should be spending any more time with a man who carries a gun under his coat and goes around whacking people."

Book looked around blankly at her. "Whacking?"

"Yes," she said, crossing her arms firmly. "And I also want to leave this city."

Book sighed wearily. "You'll be leaving soon. I promise. But Sam—"

"His name is Samuel," Rachel snapped. "Not Sam."

"Samuel," Book said patiently. "Samuel may have to come back and testify in court."

"We do not go into your courts," Rachel said. "It is not our way."

"People who don't go into our courts," Book said, "sometimes go directly into our jails."

"Do not threaten us," Rachel said. "Just let us go home."

Samuel leaned forward, whispered in his mother's ear. "What now?" Book said.

"He says you look tired. I agree."

"I am tired," Book said.

"But not a good tired."

"What the hell is a good tired?"

"Don't swear."

"Hell isn't swearing. Just the name of a place. And you didn't answer my question."

"A good tired is what you get from doing a good thing. Like plowing a field."

"I *was* plowing a field," Book said. "The South Philadelphia mine field."

"I do not think you are funny," Rachel said.

"You got to stand in line for that one," Book said.

Book, seeking to protect them from the stridency of the squad room, brought Rachel and Samuel to a conference room adjacent to his office, and had the mug books brought there for Samuel's inspection. "The black faces, Sam. That's all you've got to worry about," Book said. Then, glancing at Rachel, he said, "Samuel."

"Yes, sir," Samuel said.

Three hours later, Samuel was still turning pages, and Rachel—over against a window, doing her knitting—was looking annoyed.

"Why don't we go have some lunch," Book said.

"It's about time, John Book," Rachel said. "And not only that, I want you to show me the laws that say you can keep us here like this!"

"After lunch," Book said. "Guarantee it."

He took them to a hotdog stand opposite Independence Square. The sun had finally broken through the iron-gray sky, dried out the seat of the park bench they found near the Liberty Bell Memorial. A steady stream of camera-bearing tourists filed by the Liberty Bell, taking pictures as they went, and Samuel watched them as he downed two hotdogs heaped with sauerkraut, potato chips, two cartons of milk, and a big bag of peanuts.

"What do they think they will see?" Samuel said. "It is a bell."

"But it's the Liberty Bell," Book said. "It's a symbol of freedom, right?"

Samuel nodded, then spoke to his mother in dialect. Rachel looked at Book when Samuel was done, paused, and said, "He says he likes you."

Samuel immediately turned his face away, and Book, speaking to the back of Samuel's head, said, "I like you, too, Sam." Samuel, as if in reply, issued a resounding belch. "Well done, Samuel," Book said. "Make a cop out of you yet."

"Oh," Rachel said, "Do police also belch?"

"Never, if you want the truth. When we feel a belch coming on, we go out and shoot somebody."

Rachel smiled, in spite of her best efforts not to. "Your sister says you don't have a family."

"No."

"She thinks you should get married and have children of your own."

Book stopped in mid-chew. "She said that, did she?"

"Yes," Rachel continued, matter-of-factly, "But she thinks you are afraid of the responsibility."

"You don't say," Book said. "Anything else?"

"Oh, yes," Rachel went on cheerfully. "She thinks you like policing because you think you're right about

60

everything. And that you are the only one who can do anything. And that when you drink a lot of beer you say things like none of the other police would know from anything."

"I beg your pardon."

"Well, like the other police wouldn't know a criminal from a bag of elbows."

"Elaine said that? A bag of elbows?"

"Not exactly. But like that."

Book looked at Rachel, nodded slowly. "Glad you and Elaine got along so well."

"Oh yes. She's a good person. With fine sons."

"Ah hah," Book said, also nodding. "Let me ask you a question. You've got me all figured out now, right?"

"I think so, yes," Rachel said, very positively.

"My question is . . . why are you going to Baltimore? I mean, an Amish woman, a widow? What is it? A vacation on the Chesapeake?"

"No."

"Would you care to explain?"

"No."

"I don't mean to pry. Just curious."

"You are prying," Rachel said. "And it is none of your business."

Book nodded, let it go. This Amish woman was a very tough nut. And, Book acknowledged to himself, one of the most attractive women he had ever met.

Book was on the telephone with narcotics, discussing a two-year-old case in which he would have to testify, when he saw—through the glass partition of his office— Samuel stopping in front of a glass case at the far end of the conference room. A glass case full of various plaques, public service awards, framed newspaper accounts, and photographs of award ceremonies. A new set of mug books had been delayed, and Samuel had had time to wander around, while his mother continued her knitting near the window. But what caught Book's eye was Samuel's fascination with a particular picture.

Samuel had started to walk away, then had gone back, then had pointed to it and called to his mother—and when she had apparently not heard him—he had put his face against the glass of the case and had held it there.

"I'll have to call you back," Book said into the telephone. He hung up, walked out quickly into the conference room. "Samuel?" he said. "What is it?"

The boy was standing motionless before the glass case. He pointed. "There," he said.

"What is it, Samuel?" Rachel said, coming up.

"There, Momma," Samuel said. "That is the man."

"What man is that, Sam?" Book said. "Say it out loud for me."

"That is the man who cut the other man's throat."

"Oh, dear God in heaven," Rachel said.

"Never mind," Book said. And he looked in and read the caption under the newspaper photograph aloud. "Division Chief McFee Honored For Youth Project." Book backed away a step, nodded, muttered bitterly, "McFee. The son of a bitch."

Book rammed the car through the heavy downtown traffic with Rachel seated next to him, holding tightly to her far corner of the front seat. She stared ahead saying nothing for a far longer time than Book had thought possible, and then fairly barked out her challenge. "Why don't you arrest that man?" she snapped. "Is it because he is a fellow police?"

"Listen," Book said, more harshly than he'd intended, "I'm the cop who polices the other cops. Do you understand? I'm not in the business of protecting crooked cops!"

"Then why—"

"Because I have to know everybody involved," Book said, interrupting. "Then I'll make an arrest that'll mean something!"

"Yes, very well," Rachel said, with surprising equanimity. "But tell me, Mr. Book, why would other police murder?"

"I don't understand this, Mr. Book," Samuel said

from the back seat. "I don't understand why men of the law would kill one another."

Book heaved a great sigh. "Well, I'll tell you, Sam. Samuel. And you, Rachel. Not all men of the law are all they might be. Should be. That's what my job is all about. Keeping them in line. Trying to keep them from . . . from temptation." Book rolled his eyes upward, continued with diminished zeal. "Look, it's a narcotics operation. Dope. They make dope out of chemicals. Somehow they knew I was getting close. They knew I'd stop their selling dope on the streets. Where they make millions of dollars. Millions, and I'm not kidding. Bad cops living like rich men."

"But why would they kill people?" Rachel asked.

"They'd do anything," Book said. "Anything to keep it going."

"So they killed the police I saw?" Samuel asked.

"They killed him, Sam," Book said. "They'd kill their own mothers to keep the operation going."

"Dear Lord," Rachel said.

"And they can mostly get away with it," Book said, "because they are cops."

"I am afraid," Rachel said. "I am afraid for Samuel, and I want to go home."

"You'll be safe," Book said. "You don't have to worry."

"Oh yes!" Rachel said, exploding. "Of course! Why shouldn't we feel safe in a city where the police are so busy killing one another?"

Book started to answer, couldn't think of a rational response, let it go. Then he said, "I'll only be a minute at Schaeffer's."

Book had invariably been ill at ease at Paul Schaeffer's house. The high-middle split-level in a row of nearly identical structures. With the tidy yard and the equally tidy wife. A measure of serious equanimity was necessary for it all, Book thought, eyeing the trellis of winter-barren climbing roses next to the front door. You had to have your priorities properly reduced to live in this manner, to settle for it, to settle into it. Maybe, Book thought, Schaeffer had had this in mind all along. He hoped so. He certainly hoped so.

Marilyn Schaeffer opened the door, accepted his quick kiss on the cheek, ushered him into the living room, and sat him down, fairly gushing with affection.

As soon as Schaeffer came through the door, shut it behind him, and assumed his official pose, hands clasped behind his back, Book said, "It was McFee, Paul. Fucking medal-winning McFee."

Schaeffer stared for an instant, straightened, walked away toward the wet bar, picked up a bottle of bourbon, poured a stiff drink over ice, then looked back at Book. "You're sure?"

"I told you about the Amish boy? He nailed him like a shoe on a horse."

Schaeffer walked over, handed the bourbon drink to Book. Rock music was thundering on a stereo upstairs, and Book thought about it and then remembered the name of Schaeffer's teenage daughter. It was Kathy. "Kathy," Schaeffer said. "Loves Steely Dan."

"Right," Book said. "Admire them myself."

"Last guy I would have figured," Schaeffer said, going back and pouring himself some Scotch. "I mean, McFee was one of our prize exhibits."

"Isn't it always the way?"

"You have no doubts?"

"If I did, Paul, I wouldn't be here."

Schaeffer took a sip of his drink, then uttered an uncharacteristic oath. "Christ! Can't we ever depend upon anybody?" He walked over, opened the door, shouted: "Marilyn! Tell her to shut that thing off!" He slammed the door, turned back to Book. "One whole goddamned generation of Americans is growing up deaf. You realize that?"

"Get out of pork bellies and into hearing aids," Book said drily.

Schaeffer sat down behind his desk, sipped his drink. "Okay, tell me about McFee."

"It's almost too neat," Book said. "Four years ago narcotics confiscated five hundred and fifty gallons of the base substance P2P. Guess who was in on the collar?"

"McFee."

"Right. At the time, the street chemists knew P2P was potent, but they didn't know how to process it. They found out how to process it about six months ago. The stuff is now worth about five grand a pint. The five hundred and fifty gallons of P2P, signed for by then Sergeant McFee, disappeared two weeks after the bust. You figure it out, it comes to two million plus."

"Where's McFee now?"

"On vacation. Word is, he's heading for Florida."

"Who else knows?"

"You and me. And Carter, as far as I've filled him in."

"Okay. What are you going to need to clean it up?"

"More people. I've got to pick up where Zenovich left off. I need more people from outside the department."

Schaeffer nodded, swiveled his chair back and forth. "Okay. Maybe the Bureau. Or those DEA bastards. I'll take care of it." He turned to Book. "I'll do my part, you do yours, Johnny. Cut their balls off. I'm counting on you."

"Why not?" Book said, grinning. "I'm reliable."

"What's your first move?"

"A shower. Haven't changed clothes in two days."

After he'd dropped Rachel and Samuel off at Elaine's—over Rachel's protests about imposing, and the rest of the standard complaints—Book drove to his apartment building fairly luxuriating in the thought of that shower, that change of clothes. As he got out of his car in the cavernous parking garage, he hesitated, then reached into the back seat, and grabbed the file on McFee. The thought of reading it almost sickened him, but, when it came to business, Book was resolute. Of

65

course he would read the sports section of the Philadelphia *Inquirer* first, but one had to respect one's priorities.

He paused under a streetlight across from his apartment, reading about how the Eagles just might trade for a new quarterback, when he felt eyes on him. He looked up . . . and there was McFee, coming at him quickstep, with a big smile on his face and one hand buried in a shopping bag. Book thought, Welcome to eternity, baby. Here comes your death. And before Book could get his right hand to so much as drop the newspaper, McFee, still smiling hugely, let the shopping bag fall away, uncovering a short-barreled pistol with a silencer on it. McFee didn't miss a stride or hesitate an instant; fired right out of the middle of his smile, and kept on coming.

Book, trying to throw himself sidewise in a desperate lunge, felt the bullet drive into his belly with a fiery rush. He heard the second shot—a sound like an air gun—and was amazed at the length of time the bullet took to reach him. And he heard Schaeffer's voice asking, "Who else knows?" And he heard his own voice answering, "You and me." And he felt the sidewalk grinding into the side of his face, and he thought, Brace yourself, God. Here comes Johnny.

Then there were headlights sweeping over his face, and he thought he heard McFee's voice cursing. And he lay there, waiting to die, figuring he would soon be in that famous tunnel, with the light at the end of it, the warm light, and then Jesus coming to meet him, just as all the new-born Christian almost-dead described it on the talk shows. But it didn't happen. What happened was the beginning of the pain of it, just a hint at first, as the shock wore off, but then a rush of the damnedest pain he had ever known. He clutched at his belly, rolled over, came up against a fire hydrant. He heard the sound of tires squealing almost against his head. He told himself he had to grab the hydrant, get to his feet. He told his hands to stop grabbing at his belly and start grabbing the fire hydrant. Never mind the goddamned pain, he told his hands, I can live with it. And then he heard the voices of the man and the woman.

"My God," she said, "he's bleeding!"

"Hey, buddy," he said. "What the hell happened?"

"Nothing," Book said. "Hemorrhage. Fucking inherited hemorrhage, is all." He pulled himself to his feet, felt the blood oozing out between his fingers, tried to smile.

"Jesus, buddy," the man said. "You got to get to a hospital, inherited or not! Let me give you a hand."

"No!" his wife shouted. "You help him and you are legally responsible, Henry!"

"She's right, Henry. You wouldn't want to be legally responsible now, would you?"

"Shut up, Ramona!" Henry said. "This man's been shot."

"No, no, Henry," Book said. "Just a small leak, is all it is. Go away, Henry. Go bowling, or whatever you do."

"You see?" Ramona said. "If he wants to die in the street, it's his business, Henry."

"Hey," Henry said, turning on Ramona, "will you shut the hell up? I ain't going to let a man bleed to death!" He started toward Book. "Come on, buddy. I been through a couple of wars. I know when it's hospital time!"

Book turned on him, his .38 pistol pointed. "No goddamned hospital, Henry. You get the message?"

"Shit," Henry said. "I was just trying to help."

"You're a model citizen, Henry. Now get the fuck out of here. And take Ramona with you."

"I told you, Henry!" Ramona trumpeted.

Book staggered back toward his car, the pistol still pointed . . . because Henry was still hanging, jaw thrust, determined to do something. "I'm going to call the goddamned cops," Henry said. "I'm going to get a cop over here!"

That's right, Book thought, as he unlocked his car

and forced his body to move in behind the wheel, get to a telephone, Henry. Get to a telephone and call a cop.

Book reached into the gym bag on the seat next to him, and found a pair of dirty athletic socks—the only things he hadn't already stuffed into his wounds. He wadded them up and stuffed them home, wincing with pain, thinking that the bleeding was easing up a bit, that he wasn't going to die before lunchtime, anyway, and that God must have intended him for a higher purpose. Like blowing fucking McFee away with a ten gauge shotgun.

He eased himself out of the car and into the telephone booth with a niceness of movement dictated by agony. He dialed with the same precision.

"Good fucking morning," Carter said.

"Same to you. Now listen, Elton. Listen very carefully. I wrote the name and the address of the Amish woman on my desk calendar, in my office. I want you to go there, tonight, right now, and destroy said calendar. The whole damned calendar. You understand?"

"Sure, but what the hell are you into? What's happening?"

"You will invariably do as I say?"

"You got my solemn word."

"Good. I'm not going to be around for a while. I'll call you when I can."

"Johnny, what the fuck?"

"Listen. Take care of that desk calendar for me. And watch your touchhole. My old friend and mentor, Paul Schaeffer, is part of it. Maybe at the top of it."

"You shining me?" Carter said, genuinely shocked.

"Gospel, Elton. Get your iron pants on."

Rachel was sound asleep when Elaine came into the room. Samuel was sprawled upside down in his bed, holding Buck's toy machine gun in one hand. Elaine touched Rachel's shoulder, shook her awake. She came out of sleep smiling sweetly. "Oh, Elaine. What is it?"

"It's John," Elaine said. "He says you have to leave now. He says it is urgent."

"Urgent?"

"I believe him, Rachel. He looks awful."

"Oh. He means right now?"

"Right now."

"Very well. Tell him we'll only be a minute."

Elaine went out as Rachel began to talk Samuel out of his utter sleep.

"Put my car in the garage, and close and lock the door," Book said.

Elaine, standing outside the door of the bathroom, spoke sharply, trying to keep her voice down. "Goddamn it, John, you're hurt, aren't you?"

"Nothing I can't handle," Book said, wincing at himself in the mirror. He took a washcloth out of the hot water in the sink, wrung it out, applied it to one of the holes in his left side. Very neat holes they were, oozing blood, looking very much like all of the holes in all of the dead bodies he had ever seen. The exit holes were more ragged, but not nearly as bad as they might have been. Nice of McFee to use hard-nosed bullets. The pain was extreme, constant, rising about once every two minutes to an intensity that damned near knocked him down. He finished washing the wounds, then took one of Elaine's bath towels, wrapped it around his waist, secured it with a sash from her bathrobe, and started dressing himself as Elaine rapped sharply on the door.

"John? If you're hurt, why don't you go to a hospital?"

"Worst thing I could do. Hospitals got to report certain kinds of injuries right away. They'd track me right down."

"My God, you've been shot!"

"It isn't the first time, probably won't be the last."

"I know a doctor I can trust. He wouldn't report—"

"Forget it!" Book said, interrupting. "I'll find a

doctor later. Out in the woods somewhere. First, I got to get the boy and his mother the hell out of Philadelphia. Before they get shot up."

"I'll take them."

"No way. You're in this already too goddamned far. Just please, for fucking once, do what I say!" Book struggled into his trench coat, cinched the belt as tight as he could stand it.

"They'll be coming here, won't they?"

"Yes," Book said. "Schaeffer knows I have a sister."

"What'll I tell them?"

"You don't know anything. I borrowed your car. Didn't say why. You never heard of any Amish woman and her boy. Got it?" Book, pistol in hand, opened the bathroom door.

"My God, John, you look awful."

"Got to get me a tan one of these days."

"I can't let you do this."

"Give me your car keys, Elaine. We ain't got a whole hell of a lot of time."

Book drove across town with desperate concentration, trying to think of nothing but the road ahead. We are in motion, people, he thought. And it is necessary to stay in motion. Therefore, we will pay strict attention, not depart the highway nor wander across the white line. Twice police cars came up behind him, and he died a little, but both times they went on by without so much as a glance. Rachel, sitting next to him, had ridden in annoyed silence for the first twenty minutes, but was now getting restive, and finally spoke.

"Where are you taking us now?" she asked.

"Home," Book said.

"Lancaster County?"

"Yes, ma'am."

"Well," she said primly, "I'm very pleased to hear it. But couldn't it have waited until morning?"

"No."

"Why not?"

"Because."

"Because why?"

"Because the Holy Ghost over the bent world broods."

"I don't understand."

"Neither do I."

"You said we would be safe in Philadelphia."

"I was wrong."

"Kinner un Narre," Rachel said, shaking her head.

"What?"

"Kinner un Narre saage die Waahret," Rachel said. Then she translated for him. "Children and fools say the truth."

"You got that right," Book said. "But which one am I?"

"I think you're a little of both," Rachel said.

And he was thinking, By God, that's a good-looking woman, when the pain came up and almost took his hands off the wheel.

CHAPTER NINE

Carter signed in at the security desk without offering any explanation for his late night visit to head-quarters. The uniform on watch eyed him inquir-ingly, but offered no challenge.

Riding up in the elevator, Carter turned over in his mind the possible reasons for his partner wanting to purge any record of the Amish woman's whereabouts. All things considered, it wasn't likely Book intended to run away to Miami Beach with her. And the only alternative meant trouble on the case. Serious trouble, most likely, if Johnny didn't feel like telling him what it was all about.

That didn't surprise Carter. Something about this one had smelled ugly to him from the beginning. In fact, it was the kind of smell that made him feel relieved that he had a John Book for a partner. Book was straight, tough, and he was *there* when it counted. In fact, there were times when Carter felt it was the two of them against the world. Not that they were friends, necessarily—there were too many personality differ-ences for that—but in the kind of work they did, a sort of bunker mentality often prevailed. And that, at least in the case of Carter and Book, fueled a relationship that went deeper than friendship.

On the third floor he let himself into Book's office, and went straight to the desk calendar. He found the woman's name and address on the back of a page: Rachel Lapp, Route 3, Strasburg," tore it out, stuffed it in his jacket pocket.

He went out and was locking the door behind him when the elevator arrived at the third floor. Two men got off—two ad-vice detectives, one named Bryce, the other named Ferguson, or Fergie—and crossed quickly into the men's room without speaking to Carter.

Carter got on the elevator, and, just as the door closed, saw Bryce and Ferguson coming out of the restroom headed in the direction of Book's office. Which was strange—if not simply because forty seconds was some kind of record for using a facility— because ad-vice was at the other end of the hall.

PART TWO

CHAPTER TEN

Book, driving grimly, hands gripped fiercely to the
wheel against the pain, watched it become daylight.
He watched the sun dance ahead of him down the
blacktop of Route 30 lighting up the fields on either
side, the stubbled fields and beyond them the leafless,
black-sparred woods. He blinked at the sun as the car
approached an intersection, lifted his left foot to the
brake, groaned as the pain shot through his left side all
the way upward into his jawbone. Book baby, he
thought, you are hurt bad. He squinted to read a road
sign. It said that Kinzers was two, or three, or five miles
up the road. Rachel had said something about turning
at Kinzers. He looked across to her, and saw that she
was sound asleep. He glanced back and there was
Samuel stretched full length across the back seat, flat
on his back, his mouth open, snoring gently. Better to
wake the mother, he thought. Always better to wake
the mother.

"Rachel," he said softly.

"Yes, Jacob," she said, coming awake immediately.

"It's Book," he said. "Sorry about that."

"Oh, oh, what did I say?" she said.

"You said Jacob."

"Oh," she said, brushing at her hair with one hand. "I am sorry. I was dreaming about him. About Jacob."

"Jacob? Oh, right. Your husband."

"You called me Rachel."

"That's your name."

"So is Mrs. Lapp."

"Mrs. Lapp, we are fast approaching a place called Kinzers. I need some directions."

"You turn left at the intersection."

"I'm sorry I had to wake you."

"And I'll give you directions from there."

"Right."

She looked at him for a moment. "Are you all right?"

"I've been better."

"You look very white."

"I had a skin transplant."

"Here, here!" she said, pointing ahead. "Turn to the left here!"

"Yes, ma'am."

Book put the wheel hard over, negotiated the corner at thirty miles an hour with a small screech at the tires.

"There's no need for going speeding," Rachel said.

"Right," Book said. "Now where's the next turn?"

"Not for a little bit yet," Rachel said.

"Where are we?" Samuel said, rising up in the back seat.

"Almost home," Rachel said. "See?"

"Oh," Samuel said, looking around. "Kinzers."

"How many more turns?" Book asked sourly.

"Just one more," Rachel said. "If you will slow down."

"You mean there's more turns if I don't slow down?"

"I mean we won't make even the next one if you don't slow down," Rachel said very positively.

Book shook his head. "I was only doing thirty."

"You have been drinking I think," Rachel said. "While I was asleep."

77

Book, aching at the vitals, nodded. "Oh yeah. I've been dancing on the goddamned roof."

"Stop swearing," Rachel said primly. "Or Samuel and I will get out right here."

"Yes, ma'am," Book said. And he thought: I am starting to lose it, folks. I am definitely sliding for home.

Rachel pointed out the next turn, and Book took it, braking all the way. There were two more turns, one more of a long curve, the other a sharp right into the farmhouse lane. Book made it with considerable effort, the pain sweat breaking out all along his forehead. The road climbed a low hill, topped it, and then descended into the barnyard of the Lapp farm. At the top of the rise, Book—blinking badly now, barely able to see a hundred feet in front of him—socked the car to a stop.

"That's it?" he said.

"That is our farm," Rachel said.

"Thanks be to Jesus."

"Amen," Rachel said immediately.

Book looked at her, surprised. "That isn't swearing?"

"Not if you didn't mean it to be," Rachel said, eyeing him closely.

"Right," Book said. "Everything's relative."

"What?"

"I said God give us increase," Book muttered. He looked away to the farm, spread out below them, the white buildings gleaming in the morning sun, the white rail fences perfectly reflected in the mirror-still, iced ponds, the drifts and patches of snow shooting shafts of sunlight off their surfaces into the black leafless trees beyond—and all of it so neat, so clean, so surrounded in peace and orderliness that his heart leaped for want of it. Dear God, he thought, if I could just lie down here and soak it up and gather it in and go back. Go back and remember. That summer in Indiana. That shining summer when I was nine. Or ten. Or whatever the hell. And forget it, Book baby. You got holes in the head, and holes in the bod. And time to get this expedition in gear.

He eased the car into motion, the pain in his side and belly almost intolerable now. He set his eyes on the road, got his left foot up onto the brake pedal, and rolled down the hill at ten miles an hour. He stopped at the head of the path leading to the house, turned and looked at Rachel. "You are home," he said.

"Thank you," Rachel said, gathering up her two cloth bags.

"Thank you, Mr. Book," Samuel said from the back seat. "See you later." Samuel jumped out of the car, slammed the door behind him, and ran up the path toward the house.

Book looked after him for a moment, then turned again to Rachel. "The kid has the right idea. Get the hell away from me."

"Why, I don't believe that at all. I think he likes you."

"Right," Book said, drily. "I've been charming."

Rachel looked at him for a moment, spoke softly. "Why don't you come in the house. Rest for a time. I'll make coffee and breakfast."

Book shook his head. "Can't do it."

"You look sick."

"You got that right."

"Come in, then."

"I've got business."

"What about Samuel? Will you come back to take him to trial?"

"There isn't going to be any trial."

"I don't understand."

"You don't have to," Book said impatiently. "Now, if you'll excuse me?"

Rachel nodded, opened her door, started to slide out, then looked back at him. "I wish you good luck, John Book. And God's blessing."

"Right. Same to you."

She continued to look at him for a time, then got out

of the car and pushed the door shut very slowly, her eyes on him the whole time. "Goodbye," she said through the open window. "God go with you."

And he thought, Jesus, that's a good-looking woman. He said: "Bye, bye. Keep the faith."

He put the car in gear and started forward, not sure where he was going, but determined to go, to get away and to the nearest doctor. The car was climbing a low hill toward an intersection of barnyard trails, clearly marked in the residue of melting snow. Book gunned the engine to make the hill just as a wave of nausea rolled up from his stomach and came to rest at the back of his eyes. He coughed, tasted blood, and blacked out as he started to turn the car to avoid hitting a shed.

CHAPTER ELEVEN

Rachel walked up the path to the farmhouse, sighing as she watched Eli embrace Samuel, and heard Samuel say, "They killed a man with a knife."

"Rachel," Eli said, "What is all of this? What is the boy saying? Who is that man in the motorcar?"

"I will explain," Rachel said.

"Momma!" Samuel cried. "Look! He is crashing!"

Rachel turned to see Book's car skidding sidewise, hitting a pole with a birdhouse on top of it, and sliding off the road into a ditch just in front of the corncrib. The car bounced once, then came to a stop against a concrete drain abutment. Rachel dropped the bags and ran toward the car shouting, "Book! John Book, you stop that right there!"

"Who is that man?" Eli said to Samuel.

"He is a police cop," Samuel said. "From Philadelphia!" And he ran after his mother.

The car was at the bottom of a ditch in about a foot of old snow. Rachel slid down to the driver's side door, pulled it open, and had to catch Book to keep him from falling out into the snow. She pushed him back onto the front seat, and cried out when one of her hands came away covered with blood. "John, dear God! You're bleeding!"

Book looked at her swole-eyed. "I've been shot," he said. "Twice in the belly."

"My God in heaven! Why didn't you go to a hospital?"

"No way. Hospitals report gunshot wounds. They'd trace me."

"Never mind, don't talk." She turned and shouted. "Eli! Come help!"

"*I'm* here," Samuel said behind her. "Momma?"

"Go get a clean sheet, Samuel. Hurry!"

Samuel raced away toward the house. Rachel moved in beside Book, easing him out from under the steering wheel. She loosened the buttons of his topcoat, and began to work on the belt. Book groaned. "I have to see," Rachel said.

"You won't like it," Book said.

"I've seen blood before. And not so long ago."

"Then be my guest," Book said. "But a gutshot person ain't pretty."

"Neither is one whose head has been ground up in a sileage chopper," Rachel said quietly. "Now, turn toward me, and be quiet."

"Is the English dead?" Eli asked her, half an hour later, in the small bedroom on the first floor, as she washed Book's face and chest.

"He was close to it," Rachel said. "But he is a very strong man."

"Bullet holes?"

"Two."

"And the bullets?"

"They went on through. It must have been a very powerful gun."

"You didn't see the shooting, Rachel?"

"Of course not." She turned and looked at Eli. "If I had seen it—known of it—do you think I would have waited this long to treat it?"

Eli touched his jaws for a moment, then nodded.

82

"No, surely." He eyed her for a moment. "You will want a doctor?"

"No."

"Why not?"

"Because a doctor will have to report a gun wound. And that will give his enemies a way to find him."

"His enemies?"

"Those who shot him."

"You know these enemies?"

"No."

"They are not your enemies?"

Rachel turned toward the old man, spoke impatiently. "They are my enemies because Samuel saw what they did."

"They would come after Samuel?"

"They would kill Samuel, if they could find him."

"Mein Gott," Eli said. "What did Samuel do?"

"He witnessed a murder. In the men's room of the railroad station in Philadelphia."

"Little Samuel?" Eli said, his eyes wide, his dismay covering his face. "He saw a murder?"

"A man cut another man's throat."

"Gott in himmel. Save us, dear *Gott."*

"And it is the murderers who would come after Samuel."

"Do they know he is here?"

"Perhaps. But I do not think so."

"And the English?"

"No one followed us, Eli. We will all be safe if we keep a close walk, say nothing to anybody."

"I told Stoltzfus. He is coming."

"Stoltzfus is fine. And the elders. Any of our people. But we must be careful not to speak of this to any English."

"Who would even think of it?" Eli turned to go, then turned back. "You will explain all of this to Stoltzfus?"

"I will explain. In good time."

Eli nodded, then pointed to Book's holstered gun on a pile of Book's clothing stacked on a table next to the door. "That has no place here."

"What?" Rachel turned, a bloody cloth in her hand. "What did you say?"

"That gun of the hand. It has no place in this house."

"I know. It will go when he goes."

Eli nodded shortly, then reacted to a sharp knock at the door. He turned, pulled the door open. Stoltzfus stood out in the hallway, looking like a man much put upon.

"What is it now?" Stoltzfus said aggrievedly.

Eli scowled at him. "What it is now is what it has always been, Stoltzfus. What did you think it was?"

"I heard it was an English."

"You are right, Stoltzfus. Isn't it always an English? One way or another?"

"Are we here to exchange riddles?" Stoltzfus said, smiling.

"Come in, Stoltzfus," Rachel said. "Thank you for coming."

Stoltzfus, a short, broad, powerful man in his mid-sixties, squared his way into the room, stood for a moment looking down at Book. "Is this the English?" he asked.

"His name is Book," Rachel said.

"He looks dead already," Stoltzfus said.

"He isn't dead," Rachel said. "But he is very sorely wounded."

Stoltzfus walked over to the bed, put his hand to Book's forehead, then moved it down to his chest. "Yah," he said, after a moment. "He is burning." He nodded for a time, then turned to Rachel. "The bullets went in; the bullets went out. But there is infection. Or likely to be." He stared at Rachel. "What are you doing with an English who gets shot?"

"It is my business, Stoltzfus."

Stoltzfus regarded her for a moment, then nodded. "So, it is your business, Rachel. But it is bad business. This man will die, I think, if he don't get somehow to a hospital. Or to a doctor in town."

"He cannot go to a hospital or a doctor," Rachel

said. "He must stay here, or they will find him and kill him."

"Who is they?"

"The police."

"The police shot him?"

"Bad police. They committed a murder that Samuel witnessed by accident. They will also murder Samuel if they can find him. Mr. Book's first thought was of Samuel, to get him to safety. Mr. Book is an honest, brave man, and we owe him a great debt."

"But Rachel," Eli said, "didn't you hear Stoltzfus? He is dying."

Rachel fixed Eli with cold eyes. "Maybe he is dying. Maybe he will die here. But he will certainly die if we take him to a hospital. And then they will come for Samuel. Don't you understand?"

"But if he does die here, the sheriff will come, and he will accuse us of breaking the English laws!"

"No! We'll find a way so that no one knows."

"Rachel!" Eli barked. "This is a man's life! We hold it in our hands!"

Rachel stared at Eli for a moment, then turned to look down at Book. The sunlight flooded in at the windows, intensifying the dazzling whiteness of the room. In this whiteness, against the whiteness of the pillow and sheets, Book looked like a blood-drained corpse. Rachel spoke softly. "God help me," she said, "I know the risk. And the responsibility. But we can do no other thing."

Stoltzfus, standing stolidly, his black hat held to his chest, looked to Eli. "Rachel is right. If the boy is in danger, then we must protect him."

"And if the English dies—" Eli started.

"Then he dies," Stoltzfus said. "But we will do what we can to save him." He bent over Book, fingered the bandages, his hand hovering as if feeling for vibrations. "Rachel," he said. "Make two milk poultices. Three parts milk, two parts linseed, one part epsom salts." He looked to her. "You know how it is done."

Rachel nodded. "I will also use the herbs."

"Yes." Stoltzfus turned to Eli. "Lapp, I will have to speak to the diener on this matter."

"As you see fit, Stoltzfus."

By nightfall there was a wind up, clouting the big house with the force of a heavy, flat hand, shaking the windows, causing the lamps to flicker in the vagrant draughts. Just after full dark, Rachel came into the room with the fourth set of poultices since morning. She went to Book's bedside, turned up the kerosene lamp, and set the steaming dish containing the poultices on the bedside table. She sat down in the straight-backed wooden chair next to the bed, and regarded Book for a moment. He was sleeping flat on his back, his face perfectly composed, but his breathing some-what difficult, slightly stentorious. A handsome man, she thought, but something beyond that. An animal force about him, a fierceness she had never seen before. He was a policeman, of course, and perhaps that explained some of his belligerence, his animality. But she thought not. He was a natural, primitive man who had no reason to constrain his instincts, no reli-gious sanctions. She had no prior experience with such a man, and her reactions to him puzzled her. Why would she find such a man attractive? She had no idea—except that he did have a well-muscled, fine body. Big, powerful hands, broad shoulders, heavy legs. She had seen his legs—and the rest of his body—while putting him to bed. And she hadn't since been able to get the sight of him out of her mind.

She reached over now, pulled the sheet down from his shoulders to his waist. The two poultices—almost four hours old—were yellowed and cold. But not nearly as bloodied as the last two had been. She felt his forehead, found it cooler than she'd hoped. Stoltzfus had assured her that temperatures went up at nightfall—no medical explanation—and she felt reassured that his fever had somewhat subsided.

But a moment later, as she changed the bandages, she was brought up short and staring. Book, almost wakened by the removal of the poultices, started to groan, and then to talk in his sleep. And what came out of his mouth stunned her.

"Scumbag!" Book shouted. "You want to shoot a cop? Drop it, you cocksucker!"

Rachel staggered back, almost fell down. "Dear God," she murmured, covering her ears, turning her back.

"That's enough, Enrietto! Jesus Christ! You shot the fucker in half!"

Book, having risen up a few inches on one elbow, now fell back groaning.

Rachel stood for a moment, staring at the white wall. Then she turned, slowly, sighing. She looked to Book, thinking, He is full of fever. He doesn't know what he is saying.

She walked over, and slowly sat down again. Book's broad chest was heaving, his forehead covered with beaded sweat, as was most of his upper body. She took a washcloth from the table, dipped it in the poultice basin, wrung it out, and leaned to Book. She dabbed at his forehead, his chest, his belly—moving the sheet down below his belly button—but stopping there, the sight of him affecting her unexpectedly. She had heard the phrase "the male animal," or had read it in the Lancaster newspaper, the *Intelligencer-Journal*. A strange phrase, when she'd first thought about it, but she thought she understood it now. This was the male animal for sure, an angry man, a man pitted every day against criminals, a man who got out of bed every morning never knowing if he would be alive to return to that bed that night. What a way for a man to live. And how foreign to the way of any man she had ever known before.

Book stirred, stiffened, suddenly turned and looked

directly at her. "Who the hell are you?" he said. "Where the hell am I?"

"My name is Rachel Lapp. You know me."

"I don't know you. Go away."

"You have a fever. You don't remember."

"Fever my ass! Where'd I get a fever?"

"You were shot by a gun. Twice."

"Bullshit, lady! I never been shot in my life!" He started to sit up, issued a choked scream, grabbed at his belly, and fell back on the bed. "Jesus Christ!" he shouted. "I've been shot!"

"Lie still! You will be all right!"

Book looked at her for a long moment, his eyes full of pain. Then he appeared to faint. His eyes closed, his mouth sagged, he expelled a long, soughing snarl, and fell back on the pillow and was still. Rachel reached for his wrist, felt his pulse, and spoke aloud. "Good, good," she said. "He has the heart of a horse." And was pulling the sheet up over his chest when there was a sharp knock at the door. "Come in," Rachel said.

The door was pushed open, and there was Mary Stoltzfus, her sweet, ancient face full of compassion.

"I'm bringing the tea," she said. "Mr. Stoltzfus's tea?"

"Of course, Mary," Rachel said, getting quickly to her feet. "Please come in."

Mary came across the room carrying a large earthenware teapot. "Mr. Stoltzfus said he should have two cups before he goes to sleep. Mr. Stoltzfus says you must be firm, see to it that he drinks it all down."

"I'll be firm, Mary," Rachel said, as Mrs. Stoltzfus put the teapot down on the bedside table.

"It has been steeping for almost an hour," Mary Stoltzfus said. She smiled, nodded, and turned to go. "But," she said, turning back, "it is very bitter no matter how long you steep it. Even five minutes. I never drink it. Only Stoltzfus drinks it, once a year, for the gout. He still gets the gout, but he still drinks it once a year. Don't you drink it, dear. It tastes like bad sauerkraut."

She giggled, put her hand to her mouth, and went out. Rachel looked after her, smiling, and thought, Just the thing for him. Sauerkraut will maybe sweeten his mouth.

CHAPTER TWELVE

Assistant Chief Paul Schaeffer sat at his desk staring across the room at a wall map of Pennsylvania. *The son of a bitch is down there,* he thought. *Somewhere in Lancaster County. Tough son of a bitch, with two .38 holes in him, and no report of his going to a hospital or a doctor. You always had guts, Johnny. And I love you like a brother. But this time you came down real awkward, and you got to go.*

The telephone buzzed. He picked it up. "What have you got, Joyce?"

"I've got Undersheriff Hess," his secretary said. "In Lancaster County. The Sheriff went to Harrisburg."

"Put him on," Schaeffer said.

Undersheriff Hess came on booming. "Well, hello there, Chief. What can we do for you?"

"Well, I'll tell you, Sheriff. We got a big problem involving one of your Amish families."

"Amish? They ain't usually a problem."

"I know that. And this isn't exactly a case of their wrongdoing. Just that an Amish boy witnessed a killing up here, in the 30th Street railroad station. Maybe you read about it?"

"No, can't say as I did, Chief. But I don't get much time for the newspapers. Or the television, either."

"Right," Schaeffer said, grimacing. "Understand how it is. Busy's the name of the game."

"You can say that again."

"Listen, Sheriff, the thing is the Amish boy was with his mother, and I have her name."

"Her name? What'd you do with her herself?"

"Well, that's the problem. She and the boy took off, back to Lancaster County. Right in the middle of the investigation."

"Well, that's how them Amish are, you know. They don't hold with the legal process, the way you and I know it."

"That's what I understand. But listen, this woman, this Rachel Lapp? I'd sure appreciate your help in locating her."

"Yeah, well, that's the problem, right there, Chief. You see, we got maybe six thousand of your Amish over here. Just in Lancaster County. And if you add in—"

"I know all about that," Schaeffer said impatiently. "But I told you, I have the woman's name. Rachel Lapp?"

"You got an address?"

"No. If I had an address, I'd—"

"You got a route number, name of a road?"

"No, I don't, but—"

"See?" Hess said, interrupting again. "I mean, about every third person of your Amish persuasion is named Lapp. That or Yoder. Or Stoltzfus. I mean, there's probably one hundred and six Rachel Lapps in Lancaster County alone."

Schaeffer took a deep breath, fought to control himself. "That's very interesting, Sheriff. But we're a talking about a major crime, involving the murder of a police officer. And another police officer who was shot during the investigation. Name of John Book. We think he may have taken refuge with this Amish woman."

"That so? Sounds real interesting, Chief. Why would one of your officers take refuge?"

"It's a long story," Schaeffer said, sighing heavily. "Confidential information. But let's get back to the Amish. There must be a directory of these people somewhere."

"Sure. The tax rolls. Voter registration. But let's be up front here. I just don't have the manpower to send a deputy out to every family name of Lapp in Lancaster County. Lookin' for a Rachel. Hell, it'd take months, at least."

Schaeffer controlled his tone carefully. "Maybe, Sheriff, you could do some telephoning?"

"I could sure try, Chief," Hess said, sounding somewhat amused. "But, you see, since the Amish don't have no telephones, I wouldn't know where to begin calling."

"No telephones?"

"Don't believe in them."

"Jesus."

"God's truth."

"I know, I know. I remember reading about it." Schaeffer took the phone away from his ear, looked at it, shook his head, then put it back to his ear. "Look, Sheriff, there must be something we can do."

"Well, I might get something on local radio and television for you. Like, you know, alert the public?"

"Yeah. Sounds good."

"But then, of course, the Amish don't have radios or televisions, either. So I don't know where's the good of it."

Schaeffer barked angrily. "Are you telling me, Sheriff, that there's no way we can locate this woman? We are talking about twentieth century law enforcement."

"Now there's the crux of the thing, Chief. We're talking twentieth century, but your Amish don't live in it. They don't even think it." Hess paused to allow this to register. "Tell you this, Chief. If them Amish have taken your man in, I wouldn't want to hang by a rope until we find him."

Schaeffer fairly snarled into the telephone. "Thank you very much, Sheriff! You've been a goddamned education!"

"Right you are!" Hess bellowed back. "And anything we can do to help you find folks, you let us know!"

Schaeffer hung up, stared down at his desk for a moment. "Find? Find, you dumb bastard? You couldn't find your ass with both hands in an iron lung. With God holding the fucking flashlight!"

CHAPTER THIRTEEN

Book, lying on his back with a pillow clutched over his face, heard the voices, and thought, It's the German army. They have come to finish me off. He listened, not moving, gauging the pain in his belly, finding it much reduced. A good sign. Now, where the hell was he, and who were these Germans? He listened more closely. Now they were speaking mostly English, with an accent. A trick, no doubt, to lure him into a false sense of security. He decided to play it close to the vest. He coughed once, moved the pillow just enough so that he could peer out at the room.

What he saw was a white ceiling, four white walls, a wide-board, pegged floor highly polished, and a solid oak door in the middle of the wall directly opposite the bed. There was an oval braided rug on the floor and, on either side of the door, two straight chairs hung on the wall on hooks about six feet off the floor. No view yet of the talking men. Jesus God, Book thought, I am in some kind of a goddamned monastery. Or nut house. Who the hell hangs chairs on the wall?

He pulled the pillow down a little further, cranked his head around . . . and there they were. Four black-suited men, all with full beards, all apparently talking at once. Book stared. Then it all began to come back to him, slowly. We are in Lancaster County, folks. And these here old parties are Amishmen. Right. We are in relatively safe hands. The men went back to speaking their dialect—very close to German by the sound of it—as Book pulled himself cautiously up on one elbow, grimacing at the pain of it, and spoke loudly and with all of the authority he could muster. "Listen! Any of you people speak understandable English?"

They looked around at him as one, three of them smiling nicely. And the tallest one said, "Yes, we all do, Mr. Book. I am Bishop Tschantz, the bishop of this district. This is Stoltzfus, the healer. And these two are Erb and Hershberger, two of our preachers."

"Pleased to meet you," Book said, coughing fiercely. "But if you're here to bury me, you're by God a little premature."

"I am very pleased," Stoltzfus said. "You've been drinking my tea."

"You may be pleased," Book said. "But your tea tastes like horsepiss."

Eli, standing to one side, said, "You could show a little gratitude, Book."

"And a little respect," said Erb. "This is the bishop."

Book eyed them all dubiously. "Right," Book said. "Right on all counts. Meanwhile, I'm dying."

"No," Hershberger said. "You will probably live."

"Yes, Stoltzfus," Bishop Tschantz said. "Another Lazarus to your credit."

"He was truly touched by God's hand," Stoltzfus said, smiling. "He was all but dead."

The door opened and in came Rachel with a tray. "Well, look who's up and shining," Rachel said, putting the tray down on the bedside table.

"You look familiar," Book said. "Do I know your name?"

"My name is Rachel Lapp."

"Great. And is this your boarding house?"

"This is Eli Lapp's farm. Don't you remember?"

Book looked at her, her absolutely dead-honest eyes.

He sighed. "Of course I remember. I was just being cute."

"Cute you aren't," she said, giggling.

"Thank you. Who are they?" he asked, indicating the men, who had retired in a conversational knot to the back of the room.

"They are the leadership of the district. The diener, Bishop Tschantz, is the one with no hair on top. They decided to come see you for themselves."

"Why do I rate all this attention?"

"Your being here creates problems for us. You understand."

"Who else knows I'm here?"

"Only the elders."

"How long's it been?"

"What?"

"How long have I been here?"

"Oh. Just two days."

Book nodded. "Listen, thanks for everything, but I've got to go."

"You can't. You are too sick. Anyway, you don't have any clothes. Yours got all shot up and booghered."

"Mr. Book," said Bishop Tschantz, coming forward from the group. "You are a very lucky man to be alive."

"You got that right," Book said. "And you don't look so bad yourself. For your age."

The bishop smiled gently, glanced at Rachel, then looked back at Book. "God be with you, Mr. Book," he said softly. "We will keep you in our prayers."

Stoltzfus came forward. "Rest, Mr. Book. That's the ticket. And drink plenty of my tea."

Book, looking slightly bleary-eyed, said, "Didn't I tell you what I think of your tea?"

Stoltzfus smiled. "Yes, but I never tasted horsepiss."

Book opened his mouth to answer, couldn't find the words, grinned, and eased back on his pillow.

The men went out, and Rachel, smiling, tucked the topsheet in around his shoulders. "We are all very happy that you're going to live, John Book. If you had died, we didn't know what we were going to do with you."

"Jesus, yes, I suppose. Glad to have saved you the trouble, as it were."

"You realize you must rest a few days?"

"Can't. Got to get the hell out of here."

"Stop swearing and sleep, John Book. Or I'll feed you more of Stoltzfus's tea."

There was no immediate response. And she was not surprised to find, as she looked around, that Book was sound asleep.

Rachel came out of the bedroom, tray in hand, as Hershberger was saying: "But a gunshot wound? Very serious."

Bishop Tschantz nodded, but said, "It is not, however, for us to ask how he came to us. He is afflicted. That is enough."

"Still," Erb said, "he should be among his own people. Not here."

Rachel hesitated for a moment, then said, "He will leave us as soon as he is able. He already wants to go."

Erb gave her a dubious look, turned to Stoltzfus. "How long will that be?"

"A month, maybe six weeks. With God's healing love," Stoltzfus said. "He is a tough man."

As it happened all five men turned to Rachel for confirmation. Rachel dropped her eyes for an instant, then looked up at them boldly. "He is a very tough man," she said. "And he has earned our compassion."

No one said a word as Rachel, eyes straight ahead, passed through them and went on into the kitchen.

CHAPTER FOURTEEN

Schaeffer walked up the sidewalk reluctantly, slow-footed, eyes bent to the pavement. He stood on the porch frowning for a time before he brought himself to knock. The door was opened—snatched open—almost immediately by Elaine. She scowled at him, slammed the door, and opened it again three or four inches with the chain secured.

"What the hell do you want?" she said sourly.

"I've got to talk to you."

"Did you find him?"

"Not yet."

Her eyes narrowed. "Then get lost, you bastard." She started to shut the door.

Schaeffer quickly thrust his foot against the door. "Hold on, Elaine. I'm here to apologize. For Lieutenant McFee."

"Well, that's a start!"

"He . . . he overstated the department's position."

"He accused John of taking kickbacks! And you know—*anybody* who knows John—knows that that's a goddamned lie!"

"Of course, Elaine," Schaeffer said smoothly. "All

I'm saying is, as long as there's any question, better Johnny should come back and clear his name."

"Bullshit! Better you should get off my front porch before I get my can of mace!"

"Elaine, listen to me. I don't want to have to take you in for questioning."

"Just try it, asshole."

"Elaine, you've got his car, you were the last to see him—"

"I was the last to give a goddamn!" she shouted. "Get off my porch! I don't know where he is!"

"But . . . *but,* Elaine, please, if you had to make a guess about it?"

"About *what?*"

"About where he is?" Schaeffer pleaded. "If you had to say where he might be, what would you say?"

Elaine answered without hesitation. "I'd say he's in Saskatchewan having his tits fixed!" she shouted. And she kicked the bottom of the door so hard that Schaeffer had to snatch his foot out of the way as the door slammed shut.

A moment later in the car, Schaeffer repeated his conversation with Elaine to Lieutenant McFee. And then said: "So, that's a dead end. What about Carter?"

"Tight," said McFee, "but I'm working on him."

"Don't work, lean. Lean real hard."

"Won't help," McFee said, shaking his head. "Not with Carter. Even if he *does* know, he's hard ass all the way."

Schaeffer fairly snarled. "Then break his hard ass! And that's an order!"

CHAPTER FIFTEEN

Samuel came into the room with a fresh bedpan, looked at Book lying asprawl and sound asleep on the bed, put the bedpan down on the floor, and went directly to the clothes closet. He opened the door, and stood staring at what he saw—what he knew he'd see—Book's .38 caliber revolver lying atop Book's folded clothes. He reached in, touched it, pulled his hand back at once, glanced quickly at Book. Book had not moved. Samuel gathered himself, reached in, picked the pistol up in both hands. He turned to give himself room, slowly brought the pistol up, aimed it at the pitcher on Book's bedside table. And he had just softly said "Pow" when he saw that Book's eyes were open, coldly fixed upon him.

"Give me that," Book said. Samuel, big-eyed and staring, hesitated. "Come on, bring it here, kid," Book snapped.

Samuel moved slowly across to the bed, holding the pistol barrel-down in front of him. Book took the pistol by the muzzle, pulled it out of Samuel's hands. "I was only looking," Samuel said.

Book, grimacing slightly, snapped the cylinder open, dumped the cartridges out into his hand, slapped the cylinder shut again. "You were aiming a loaded gun, Sam. Shouldn't do that."

"No, sir."

"Not unless you mean to fire it."

"Yes, sir."

"You ever handle a pistol before?"

"No pistol. Ever."

"Tell you what, Sam," Book said, gritting his teeth as he turned a bit to face the boy, "I'm going to let you handle this one. But only if you promise not to say anything to your momma. I've got a feeling she wouldn't understand."

"Okay, Mr. Book," Samuel said, grinning.

"Call me John." Book held the pistol up, pointed out the parts. "Hammer, cocked hammer, trigger, safety, safety on, safety off, fire." The hammer clicked down, Book spun the gun once around on his index finger, presented it handle first to Samuel.

"Wow," Samuel said. He reached for the handle with both hands, took it hesitantly, and pointed it straight at Book.

Book backhanded the barrel away from him, smiling. "Sam, boy. You don't want to go pointing that at people. Especially people you just started calling by their first name."

"Sorry," Samuel said. He turned in a slow arc until he had the pistol pointing at the door. He needed both thumbs to cock it, steadied it up and pulled the trigger just as the door opened and Rachel walked briskly in. She stopped short, staring wide-eyed.

"Samuel! Put that awful thing down!"

"Yes, Momma."

"And wait for me outside!"

Samuel dropped the pistol on the bed, turned, and walked from the room muttering, "I'm sorry, Momma."

Rachel waited until Samuel was gone, then turned on Book. "John Book, I would appreciate it if, during the time you are with us, you would have as little to do with Samuel as possible."

101

Book frowned at her. "Nobody meant any harm. The boy was curious. And I unloaded the gun."

Rachel hesitated, seeing that he was obviously hurting from his wounds. She softened her tone. "It isn't just the gun. Don't you understand? It's you. What you represent. The anger and violence and hatred I saw in Philadelphia." She shook her head. "That's not for Samuel."

Book looked at her thoughtfully, then nodded. "Okay. Right."

"Please, it has nothing to do with you personally."

"I understand." He picked up the bullets, handed them to her, and then gave her the pistol handle first. "Put it back in its holster, and put it where Samuel won't find it."

"I will." Rachel crossed to the clothes closet, found the holster, put the pistol in it, dropped the bullets in her apron pocket, then looked at Book. "You are comfortable?"

"Reasonably. Got a clean bedpan."

"Good. I will see you at dinnertime." She started out, holding the holstered pistol in front of her as if it smelled bad.

"Hey," Book said, as she reached the door. Rachel turned. "Friends?"

Rachel looked back at him, her face still set in annoyance. But he was smiling—a bit sadly, his pain still showing—and she smiled back, nodding. "Friends," she said, and she opened the door and went quickly out.

The holstered pistol and the bullets lay on the center of the dining table, directly under the hanging gas lamp. Eli sat at the head of the table, reading his German Bible to himself. Samuel came in with a bucket of coal, and set it down by the stove. He turned, started to speak to Eli, but didn't speak when he saw the pistol at center table. He looked at it, looked away, looked back—and locked eyes with Eli.

"Come here, Samuel," Eli said. "Come and sit."

Samuel went over, pulled out a chair, and sat down as Eli slapped his Bible shut. "Goodnight, grossfather," Samuel said.

"Samuel," Eli said. "I have a thing to tell you." He paused, pulled twice at his nose, then pointed a battered, slightly crooked forefinger at the pistol. "This gun, this gun of the hand, is for the taking of human life. Do you know that?"

"Yes, grossfather."

"Would you take a human life, Samuel? Would you kill another man? Eh?"

"I would only kill a bad man."

Eli leaned forward, extended his hands almost ceremonially. "Only a bad man. I see. And you know these bad men on sight? You are able to look into their hearts and see this badness?"

"I can see what they do," Samuel said. He turned, looked Eli straight in the eyes. "I have seen it."

"I know you have," Eli said softly, "but you must understand. What you take into your hands, you take into your heart. Having seen what they do, would you become one of them? The hand leads the arm leads the heart . . . and you have gone amongst them. Do you see?"

"Yes."

Eli paused for a moment, then spoke very quietly. "Wherefore come out from among them and be ye separate, saith the Lord. Do you hear that, Samuel?"

"Yes, grossfather."

"And," he said, pointing at the pistol, "and touch not the unclean thing!"

The old man finished somewhat loudly, his eyes fierce with intensity. He reached out with one gnarled hand, and brushed pistol, holster and bullets to the floor. He stared, glitter-eyed, for a moment at Samuel, then lowered his eyes and quietly said, "Amen."

CHAPTER SIXTEEN

S pring came suddenly to Lancaster County, out of
the end of the dark and blowing month of April, surprising the land with its light and warmth. The thaw
brought the fields to quick flood, and the sun dried
them within seven days. Eli and Samuel had the teams
out on the eighth day, the same day that the waterwheel began to turn in the pond in front of the house,
and the same day that Book finally forced himself to his
feet and took four steps to the window.

He pushed a straight chair into position, sat down
heavily, and stayed there for two hours, looking out.
Watching the sun melt the last of the ice, watching the
birds work at their nests, watching the breeze bend the
branches of the cherry tree, and watching the earth
begin to glisten and come alive under the insistent
warming of the afternoon sun. Book thought: Jesus—
and I mean that sincerely—what in hell have I been
doing with my life? Pounding salt into the ass end of
crime in Philadelphia? Christ. Might as well pound salt
into the bottom of the Great Salt Lake. I am, Lord, so
far an essay in futility. I've got to get back there and
pound one last liter of salt. But I swear to you, dear
God, that I will immediately thereafter reassess my

assets, and review my sorry situation. And I thank you, with all that I can herewith muster, for the epiphany. Or whatever the hell it was that James Joyce called it. Amen.

He was still sitting there, half asleep, when Rachel came knocking and bustling into the room. Book was nodding over a lapful of magazines—most of them copies of *The American Dairyman*—and newspapers—most of them copies of the Old Order Amish organ called *The Budget*. He snapped awake, looked around at her somewhat guiltily as she dropped a pile of old clothing on the dresser, and smiled sweetly. "Well," she said, "you have indeed risen."

"It wasn't easy," Book said. "With all the god-damned birds singing."

"Don't blaspheme."

"Right. Sorry about that. Goddamned awful habit."

Rachel shook her head. "You just swore again."

Book sighed. "I really am sorry. Won't happen again."

"Very well." She looked at his reading matter. "You've been learning things?"

"Oh yeah. I'm a real expert on manure."

Rachel giggled. "Don't be so sure. It takes a long time."

Book grinned, pointed at the clothing. "What've you got there?"

"Well," she said, "I never could get the bloodstains out of your shirt and jacket. They're *still* soaking. So I thought you could wear these." She held up a jacket and a pair of pants, both black, both of roughly cut heavy cloth.

"Your husband's?"

"Yes. It's good that someone can have the use of them. Besides, in your clothes you'd stand out to strangers."

"Good thinking."

"I should tell you," she said cheerfully, "that these do not have buttons." She moved toward him, indicating the front of the jacket. "See? Hooks and eyes."

"No buttons? Something wrong with buttons?"

"Buttons are *hochmut*," she said.

"*Hochmut?*"

"Vain, proud," Rachel said matter-of-factly. "Such a person is *hochmutsnarr*. He is not plain."

Book nodded, grinned. "Anything against zippers?"

Rachel looked away, refolded the jacket. "You make fun of me. Like the tourists."

"The tourists?"

"They will be here soon. Driving by all the time. Even coming into the yard. Some of them very rude. They seem to think we are quaint."

"Really? I can't imagine why."

"See what I say? You make fun of me."

"I would never do that, believe me."

She looked at him, held his gaze. "I believe you, Mr. Book."

"Call me John."

"All right. Then you call me Rachel."

"I will. And thank you."

"You are welcome. And you are funny."

"Funny?"

"Yes. You are so . . . so formal for an English."

Book shook his head. "I'm not trying to be formal, for an English. I'm trying to be proper, for an Amish."

She laughed delightedly. "Everything's gotten all booghered backwards!"

Book looked at her steadily, fondly. "You're a beautiful woman."

Rachel stiffened, looked away. "Mr. Book."

"John."

"Well."

Book took in a deep breath. "Okay. Could you please direct me to a telephone?"

She hesitated, then glanced around at him chin high. "Telephone," she said, flat-voiced. "Well, the Fishers across the creek. They're Mennonites. They have cars and refrigerators. And telephones in the house, even."

"No," Book said. "I'd want a public telephone."

"Oh," Rachel said, eyeing him. "Well, the store at

Strasburg." She frowned, looked away, nodded briskly. "But you won't be going into Strasburg for a while."

"I'm going this morning."

"But you aren't well enough. Stoltzfus said two more weeks."

"I know what Stoltzfus said."

"Oh," she said quietly. "I see."

"I feel fine."

"You don't look fine."

"I got secret reserves of strength."

"Yes. Well, you could go with Eli. He is taking Samuel to school. But you'll have to hurry."

"I'll hurry."

Rachel smiled, started for the door, and stopped. "I can't wait to see you Amish." She went out, grinning, then stuck her head back in again. "And I have a hat for you!"

"Thank you, Rachel," Book called, and he thought she was gone, hadn't heard. But an instant later she put her head back in at the door.

"You're welcome, John," she said, and slammed the door shut after her.

Book, feeling odd, even a little ridiculous, came into the kitchen slowly, tentatively, still finding his legs, still fighting his wounds. He stopped short, braced himself on the table, looked to where Rachel was pumping water into the sink. "Excuse me," he said.

Rachel turned, looked at him. Looked at him for a long, beaming moment. "You look plain," she said.

"Never felt plainer in my life," Book said. "I think it's all in the buttonhooks."

"I cannot believe how well you look, how fast you have recovered."

"Had a great nurse," Book said.

"I have your hat," Rachel said, taking a flat-brimmed Amish black hat from a hook behind the kitchen door. "I think it will fit."

Book took the hat, put it on, cocked his head in a pose. "Feels right."

"It's perfect!" Rachel said. "Made for you!"

"Thank you," Book said. "Almost ready for town. All I need now is my pistol."

"What?"

"My pistol," Book said. "I can't go out in public without it."

Rachel looked at him, blinking. "Are you serious?"

Book looked back at her in honest surprise. "Am I serious? Where'd you get that line?"

Rachel looked at him blankly. "A simple question."

Book nodded, smiling. "I'll give you a simple answer. I never go anywhere without my pistol."

"Dear Lord, why?"

"To protect myself."

"It didn't protect you from getting shot."

"Good point. But that was my fault, not my pistol's."

"That is nonsense."

Book cocked his head, nodded. "You may well be right, but I still want my pistol."

"Very well." Rachel went to a cupboard, reached to the highest shelf, took down the holstered pistol, handed it to Book. Book took it, loosened his belt, pushed the holster around to the small of his back, refastened the belt. Rachel observed the process with a pained eye, spoke with a slight tinge of disdain. "So? Nobody can see it."

"That's the idea."

"Why is that the idea? If nobody knows you got it, what good does it do you?"

"I don't want to scare anybody. It's just there when I need it."

"An Amish with a hidden gun of the hand. It does not look."

"I won't tell anybody. But I would like the bullets."

"What?"

"The bullets."

"Oh yes, the little things." She turned, took down a cannister from over the stove, shook the bullets out on the counter. Book picked them up, took out the pistol, loaded it. Rachel watched, fascinated. "Do they make a very loud noise?"

"Very loud. Especially if they're coming at you."

"Yes, you know about that."

"I'm an expert."

"How are your wounds today?"

"Stiff, scabby. Like me."

"You walk a little stiff. Maybe you could use a cane?"

"Maybe. You got one?"

"Yes, here." She turned, reached into the broom closet, brought out a thorn walking stick. "It was Eli's. He used it two summers ago after Luke kicked him in the kneecap."

"Luke? I thought Amishmen were peaceful."

"Luke is a mule," Rachel said, laughing. "But an Amish mule."

Book stood watching her laugh. Then, softly, he said, "You're a beautiful woman."

Rachel blinked, absorbed the compliment, and reacted briskly. "You go now. Eli is waiting."

Book nodded, took the walking stick from her, tried it out for a couple of steps, then turned, and grinned back at her. "That Amish enough for you?"

Rachel smiled, nodded. "Just keep the gun in your pants."

"Right," Book said. "God, yes." And he went out shaking with laughter.

CHAPTER SEVENTEEN

S amuel required a lift to school because of his two rabbits, Oberg and Bishop Lichtfuss. They were in a wood and wire cage too heavy for Samuel to carry any great distance. Oberg was extremely pregnant, and, as Samuel explained to Book, with any luck the birth of the new rabbits would be observed at the schoolhouse. The thing of it was, Samuel said, he wasn't at all sure that Bishop Lichtfuss—a big, pouchy-faced, very lazy rabbit—was the father. Samuel thought that perhaps Fast Walpot, his beautiful white rabbit, got to Oberg before Bishop Lichtfuss did. He'd found Fast Walpot in with Oberg one morning and, although Oberg and Fast Walpot ordinarily didn't get along at all, they'd both looked very content on that particular morning.

Book listened to all of this with a straight and solemn face, gave it as his opinion that Bishop Lichtfuss certainly didn't look like a rabbit anticipating paternity, and that anything called Fast Walpot probably did have the inside track. Samuel said they'd just have to wait to see what came out in the litter: any white rabbits, and Fast Walpot would have to take up his fatherly duties.

After they'd dropped Samuel and the rabbits at the schoolhouse—and Book had been introduced to Miss Stoltzfus, the shy, sweet-faced teacher—Book and Eli drove on into Strasburg. On the way, Eli told Book about the buggy horse, whose name was Tittle, and why he was Eli's favorite "small" horse.

"You see, a small horse is one about ten hundred pounds. Shouldn't be no more than that."

"Why not?"

"Because you want the horse lively, quick on its feet."

"High-stepping?"

"You could say that, yes," Eli said. "Like a race horse. Tittle was a trotting horse when he was young."

"Where'd you get him?"

"I got him—no, Jacob got him—from Daniel Hochleitner." He glanced at Book. "You know, the one who looks to marry Rachel?"

"Marry Rachel? Your Rachel?"

"Our Rachel. In good time, but it looks."

Book frowned. "Don't believe I've met him."

"No, maybe not. He's tall, skinny, blond-headed, and kind of long-faced. He helps out a lot, but he don't fool nobody. He's got his eye on Rachel."

"A little indecent, isn't it? This soon after her husband's death?"

"What's indecent? You think Jacob wants her to stay alone?"

"Jacob?"

"My son."

"Right. I forgot. Sorry about that."

"Well, you think a girl like Rachel should stay alone?"

"No. I just think your neighbor, Hochlight, is rushing things a little."

"Hochleitner. And he is not. He hasn't even been around much lately."

"Well, then," Book said. "I just wouldn't want to see her rushed into anything."

Eli eyed him slyly. "You wouldn't want? You are speaking for Rachel, Mr. Book?"

Book looked at Eli, looked away. "She's a friend of mine."

Eli nodded, smiled. "You are a funny English."

Book grinned. "Is that what I am? Well, I've been called worse."

Book, having gotten himself a beer at the convenience store—an embarrassing moment, with the clerk saying that he supposed that even the Amish got thirsty—and having wrapped it in a brown paper bag, finally took possession of the pay telephone at one corner of the store's front porch. Eyeing the milling tourists and hoping that none would approach the phone, he dialed, put in the necessary coins, listened as the number rang.

"Carter?"

"Book? Is that you?"

"The very same."

"Jesus, where the fuck you been?"

"Never mind that," Book said. "I'm coming in to take care of business."

"No, baby," Carter said. "You ain't coming in. Too hot. Don't come anywhere close. They're waiting for you."

"I'll bet they are," Book said. "And I'm warming to them, the sweethearts."

"Listen, Johnny," Carter said urgently. "Don't be stupid, don't be a fool. You couldn't get within a half mile of Schaeffer right now. Stay put. But stay in touch. I'll let you know when it gets reasonable."

"Right."

"You listening to me?"

"I hear you talking."

Carter sighed heavily. "Goddamn it, Johnny, where are you? I mean, where are you at?"

Book rolled his eyes upward, looked at his own

reflection in the glass of the phone booth. "Where I'm at," he said, "is maybe 1890."

"Say again?"

Book smiled. "Make that 1790."

"What'd you say?"

"I said watch your ass, man," Book said. And he hung up.

CHAPTER EIGHTEEN

Book sat on the front porch in a rocking chair, telling himself that he was about to get up, do some stretching exercises, find something to do, make himself useful. He could see, on the hillside to the south of the barns, Samuel up on the high seat of a disc harrow driving a five-mule team back and forth across a field. Out along the driveway, Eli, in his summer straw hat, was painting the fence with great energy. And down in front of the house, Rachel worked at clearing the truck garden of last year's weeds. Only Book was unemployed, and unemployable, and it rankled. He was still hurting, still had a few weeks of waiting for his body to heal itself, and he knew it. But the waiting and the idleness were wearing very heavily upon him.

And he had just about decided to get up and take a turn around the barnyard when he saw a buggy topping the rise, coming in along the driveway. Ah, Book thought, we have a diversion. We will hold our position and allow it to reveal itself. It was a bachelor or courting buggy with no top and a single seat. The driver had long blond hair, no beard, and wore his summer straw at a rakish angle. A real sport's what we have here, folks, Book told himself. Probably selling hymn-books and Stoltzfus's fucking horsepiss tea.

The driver of the buggy waved and shouted greetings at Eli, and pulled the buggy up at the head of the path to the house. He alighted, and came toward the house with a loping, graceful stride and a grin the size of a saucepan. A handsome, self-possessed young man in his early thirties. Lance Alworth, Book thought. A wide receiver if I ever saw one.

"Hello," the young man said. "I am Daniel Hoch-leitner."

"Oh yeah," Book said, taking his hand and shaking it carefully. "I've heard about you."

"I haven't been around much since the snow melted."

"Something to do with your water level?" Book asked, managing not to smile.

"No, no. Just busy. Had to get ready for planting."

"Oh, right. We all got to get ready for planting, sooner or later. Pre-planning is best. Pre-need's even better."

Hochleitner looked at him closely, eyes puzzled. "You're the Yankee, ain't you?"

"Yankee? I thought I was the English."

"Yankee, English. It's the same. But the way you're dressed all plain, I wasn't just sure."

"I haven't been sure in weeks."

"You look good," Hochleitner said genially. "Good and plain."

"Can't tell you how glad I am to hear it," Book said. "Just so long as I don't look humble."

"I don't know about humble," Hochleitner said, looking around. "I came to see Rachel."

"Can't argue with your logic," Book said drily. "Rachel's down around the corner, pulling weeds. Or something."

"Thank you, Book."

"You're probably welcome," Book said. "How'd you know my name?"

"Oh, you're famous by now," Hochleitner said, grinning. "For one thing and another."

"Don't get familiar," Book said. "Us famous people can't stand familiarity."

"You talk funny," Hochleitner said, still grinning. "But I like you, Book. You got a good face."

Book nodded, started to answer, then didn't. He simply smiled up at Hochleitner, and nodded as the Amishman moved away. You've got a good face, Danny boy, he thought. Got to keep my eye on you.

Book, finally taking his walk, glanced back toward the house, saw Daniel Hochleitner and Rachel on the porch, Rachel pouring something from a pitcher into glasses. He leaned on his cane, turned away, and found that he was looking directly into the eyes of a giant sow. The sow looked at Book for a moment, then bent its mouth to the trough, and came up chomping on a corncob and cabbage slops. Book looked at the sow sour-eyed, then said, "Pig," and limped off toward the main barn.

The barn was superheated, and the strong aroma of hay was overpowered by the even stronger smell of manure coming through the trapdoors from the lower barn. Book stood for a time in mid-barn sniffing, thinking about morgues. "Morgues I have known," he said aloud. "Story of my goddamned life."

He crossed the barn floor to an open door, and looked in. It was a workshop, an entire wall of it hung with woodworking tools. He entered, inspected the tools. They appeared to be of the finest manufacture, with blades shining and oiled, and perfectly fitted handles of polished hardwood. Book, whose father was a cabinetmaker, stood staring for a time. Somebody, he thought, knows from tools. He walked over, took a wood chisel from its place on the wall, tested the edge, nodded. Somebody, he thought, knows from edges.

He was inspecting a brad point wood drill bit with admiration—was in fact inspecting a collection of them

116

—when Rachel walked into the room. She smiled at him, and leaned against the workbench.

"Are you looking for the birdhouse?"

"Birdhouse?"

"The one you knocked down with the car."

"I knocked down a birdhouse?"

"I thought I told you."

"No. Where is it?"

Rachel looked around, spotted it behind the door. "There it is. Eli said it needs a new roof."

Book inspected it, nodded. "I'll fix it. If I can borrow some of these fine tools?"

"Of course. They belong to Eli. He's the best carpenter in the district."

"Well, I can see he's particular about his tools, so I'd better ask him first. I also want to do some work on the car."

"I didn't know you were handy."

Book picked up the bird house, set it on the bench, inspected the damage. "I did some carpentry summers while I was going to school."

"I never would have suspected," Rachel said, smiling. "Do you do anything else?"

Book glanced up at her, a touch annoyed. "Anything else? I can whack people. I'm hell at whacking."

"Whacking is not of much use on a farm."

"Now, wait a minute. There's a lot of people who think being a cop is a a legitimate job."

"I'm sorry. I'm sure it is. And," she said, giving him a long, appraising look, "I'll let those pants out for you tonight."

The way she said it seemed to Book to have the slightest sexual overtone. He eyed her closely, but she kept her eyes averted. "What happened to Hochleitner?"

"Oh, we had some lemonade, and he left."

"A real fireball."

"He said he'd talked to you. He likes you."

"I'm a likeable fellow."

"And what do you think of Daniel?"

Book looked up at her again. "I think he's after your bod."

"My what?" Rachel said, blinking innocently. Then she made the translation. "Oh, really, I . . . well, I'll see you later." And blushing prettily, she hurried out.

Book looked after her, grinning. If I had world enough and time, lady, he thought, I'd give old Hotlight a little competition.

A couple of hours later, Book was out in the upper barn working on the car. He'd discovered that the battery was dead, and he was rigging jump cables between the battery in the Lapp buggy (used to power safety lights for driving the buggy at night) and the car. He had his head in under the hood, hammering at a battery terminal with a pair of pliers and swearing loudly, when Eli came up behind him.

"Ach, Book," Eli said. "That language!"

Book, startled, raised his head, banged it against the hood of the car, and let out a yowl. "Jesus Christ!" he shouted. "Don't sneak up on a man!"

Eli took a step backwards, staring as Book did a couple of turns while holding both hands to his head. "I did not sneak up. And you ought to be ashamed, Book. Ashamed of such language, the name of the Lord."

"Yes, yes, right," Book said. "But first, is my head bleeding?" He bent his head for Eli's inspection.

"No blood," Eli said.

"Damn wonder," Book said.

"What are you doing, anyway, with my buggy?"

"Just . . . just tapping the battery a little. Mine's dead."

"You wouldn't kill mine?"

"No chance. Just borrowing a little power."

Eli nodded, snorted softly. "Well, if you are well enough to do this thing, maybe you can do work for me."

"Sure. I was thinking the same thing myself. What'd you have in mind?"

Eli shrugged. "Maybe milking."

"Milking," Book said. "Milking what?"

"Cows? You know cows?"

"I've seen pictures," Book said drily.

"Good," Eli said. "You start tomorrow morning."

"You got it," Book said.

"Also tomorrow is preaching service, Book. I think, if you want to come, I can get the diener to let you in."

"Preaching service?"

"What you English call church."

"Oh. Well, Eli, if it's all the same to you, I'll pass."

"All right," Eli said, snorting. "We worry about your soul later. Tomorrow morning, you remember the milking!"

"You got it," Book said, repeating himself.

"I just hope you got it, Book," Eli said. And he turned and walked out.

Now, Book thought, just what the hell did he mean by that?

CHAPTER NINETEEN

Book found out early the next morning.
He was awakened by a noise somewhere in the house, reached out for his watch, took a look at it. It read four thirty-three. Book groaned, put it back on the bedside table, rolled over, stuck his head in under his pillow. Then he heard something at the door. He peered out from the pillow's edge, and saw Eli coming into the room with a lantern in one hand. Eli did not stand on ceremony. He strode over to the bed, hit Book a thump in the small of the back, and said, "*Veck ouf!* Time for milking!"

Twenty minutes later Book stood blinking and yawning as Samuel slammed the stanchions shut on the six milk cows, and Eli came out of the milk house with three steel buckets in hand.

"Come on, Book," he said. "The cows are waiting."

"You mean you don't have milking machines?" Book asked, following Eli to the first cow.

"Who needs machines with only six cows?" Eli said.

"*I* wish we had machines," Samuel said. "And it's more sanitary."

"Listen to him," Eli said. "Sanitary. Never mind

sanitary, take your bucket." He handed one bucket to Samuel. "Come on, Book. I'll show you which end." Book went in alongside the first cow. Eli put a stool down. "Sit," he said. Book sat. "Now, put the bucket there, between your legs. Yes. Now reach in, take one of these, lift up with the thumb loose, tighten the thumb, pull down." A squirt of milk came out of the teat, hit the bottom of the bucket with a ringing sound. "What do you think, Book?"

"I think I'm going to throw up," Book said.

"Never mind! Grab on there!"

Book grabbed a teat, pushed up, squeezed. Nothing came out. "Gone dry," Book said.

"Didn't you hear me, Book? I said pull! You never had your hands on a teat before?"

"Not one this big," Book said grimly.

"Hah!" Eli said, starting to laugh. "Hah!" he said again, delivering a thump to Book's near shoulder that almost knocked Book off the stool. Eli managed to say, "You are a funny man!" Then he went staggering and snuffling off, beating on his milkbucket with one hand, as Book, still not fully awake, looked after him in some surprise.

"Hey!" Book shouted after him. "What do I do with this cow?"

"Milk it, Book! Milk it!" Eli managed to say, before he sat down on a hay bale and gave himself over entirely to hilarity.

That evening at dinner, Book—who had spent most of the day resting from his labors in the dairy—didn't have much appetite. The food was, as always, incredibly abundant, beautifully prepared. The Amish ate well, and Rachel was an excellent cook. But to Book—who was a bachelor and used to fast foods on the run at odd hours—the three-times-a-day regular feedings were too much, too often. His hesitance was noticed almost immediately.

"Book," Eli said, waving his fork admonitorily, "eat up. You have no appetite?"

"I'm eating," Book said, chewing determinedly. "I'm just not used to so much."

"Of course you aren't," Rachel said sympathetically. "You have to be raised on a farm."

"Not used to hard work," Eli snorted. "That's his trouble."

"I'm no cow milker, I'll give you that," Book said sourly.

"But John is a carpenter," Rachel said brightly. "He's going to fix the birdhouse."

"Is this true?" Eli asked.

"If I can use some of your tools," Book said. "Great tools."

"You know tools?" Eli said, brightening.

"You have the best," Book said. "All I need's a hammer, a draw shave, a couple of planes. Just to make new shingles."

Eli fairly beamed. "You use them, Book. You know tools." Eli looked delighted, and, as Book tried to eat some more, he eyed him closely. "Book, listen, you know a little carpentry, maybe you'd like to go to Zook's barn-raising? Eh?"

"Sure."

"Then we'd see how *good* a carpenter? Eh?"

"I guess we'd see."

"I don't know, Eli," Rachel said. "Barn-raising is very hard work. Are you sure you're strong enough?"

"No," Book said flatly. "But I wouldn't miss it. What can happen? The barn falls down?"

Eli laughed. "Good, Book! We'll see how you do."

"It's very hard," Rachel said to Book. "Climbing all over."

Book nodded to reassure her. "I'll be fine. I'll even drink some more of Stoltzfus's tea."

Rachel smiled at him, got up from the table. "I'll fix it," she said, "if you'll drink it."

Book nodded, thinking that, somehow, it was the sexiest thing a woman had ever said to him.

CHAPTER TWENTY

Book returned to his car after supper, and finally got the jump cables working. The engine didn't turn over until the fourth try, and when it did start it sounded definitely troubled. Book let it run anyway, long enough to charge the battery, then shut it down and started to work on the carburator. He had it fairly well dismantled, his head down in the engine, when he heard a noise behind him. He started to move, caught himself, and said, "Eli, if that's you, I'm going to feed you the goddamned fan belt!"

"John!" Rachel said. "That's blasphemy!"

Book turned, glowered at her. "I have precedent and good cause! Eli sneaked up on me yesterday, and I damned near brained myself!"

"But that is no excuse for the taking of the Lord's name!" Rachel said, speaking with such intensity that Book had to yield.

"Right," he said. "You're right."

"It is, perhaps, one thing on the streets of Philadelphia, but it is quite another thing here. I hope you agree, John."

"I agree," Book said quickly. "Doing my best to reform. As God is my next witness."

"You're making fun again."

"No, no, I swear. I'm giving it my best shot," Book said, but he was grinning as he said it.

"Well, I see you're working on the engine. When will you be going?"

"Not long. A couple of weeks, maybe less. Soon as I stop leaking around the edges."

"You've got to be careful. We don't want any infection."

"You wouldn't believe how careful I'm being. Why the furthest I've been in any direction is Strasburg. And you can't hardly get infected in Strasburg."

"Stop making fun, or I'm going back to the house."

"Wait," Book said. "I've got a surprise for you." Book walked over to the driver's side door, reached into the car and turned on the radio. At first there was an announcer talking about used cars. Book turned the dial, and there was a whining young man's voice singing about how he knew nothing about geography, biology, or anything else. Book turned up the sound, turned to Rachel, shook his head in admiration, and said, "Oh now there, *there* is one of the best songs of the last twenty *years*."

"Dear Lord," Rachel said, listening. "You can't be serious."

"There you go again," Book said. "Of course, I'm serious. Listen."

The young man, singing through his nose, went on to say how he didn't know much about anything at all, except that he did know he loved his girlfriend. Rachel listened, and then said, "He sounds like a braying idiot to me."

"Just listen to the music," Book said. "Never mind the words."

"He sounds like a braying idiot anyway," Rachel said. "Why would anybody sing such a thing?"

"Would you just listen to the rhythm?" Book said, getting a bit annoyed. "I mean, it's just a damned classic, is all."

"No need to swear."

"I didn't swear! I said damned."

"I think I'll go into the house."

"Rachel!" Book shouted, annoyed. "I'm sorry I said damned, or damn, or whatever the hell. But would you please relax, I mean, just relax, and listen to the music?"

Rachel hesitated, then smiled. "All right, I will listen. For just a minute. But I don't much like English music."

"Will you just listen?" Book said, straining to keep his voice down. "For the sake of intra-cultural harmony?"

"I will listen for your sake," Rachel said.

"Thank you," Book said, and the words were no sooner out of his mouth than the song ended. "Oh, for God's sake!" he said.

"You're taking the name of the Lord in vain," Rachel said sternly.

"Not in vain," Book said. "Not at all. It does me a lot of good to—wait, wait. Listen! That's the Mamas and the Papas! 'California Dreamin'!"

Book started to mouth the words and move with the music. He reached into the car, turned the radio up almost all the way. The sound of the music filled the barn. Book turned, danced back toward Rachel, smiling and singing. Rachel put her hands over her ears, started to protest, then started to laugh as Book came up. "Please!" Rachel said loudly. "Eli will hear!"

"You like it, don't you?" Book said, "I can see you like it."

"No, no," she said, laughing.

Book reached out, took her by both hands, eased her into the dance. She was a study in approach-avoidance, starting to move, then pulling back. "You're feeling the music," Book said. "Look at you go. Next you'll be drinking beer and riding motorcycles."

"No, I won't," Rachel said. "That's enough, now. Let me go."

"We're just getting started!" Book said, pulling her to him for the first time. "Relax and enjoy!"

"Rachel!" Eli shouted from the barn door. "Rachel, you stop that right now!"

Book and Rachel turned to see the old man glowering at them, face like a thunderclap. Rachel immediately broke away, walked past Eli scowling right back at him. "This is none of your business," she said sharply.

Eli turned, stared after her. "Shame on you!" Then he turned back to Book. "And you, too, Book!"

Book, already at the car, reached in and turned the radio off. He looked at Eli, didn't say a word. Eli turned and stomped away after Rachel. Book leaned on the car door, hung his head. Well done, Ambassador Book, he thought. You have just re-established relations with the seventeenth century.

He was just setting foot on the front porch, lantern in hand, about ten minutes later when he stopped short at the sound of Rachel's voice coming from the kitchen.

"I am not ashamed of anything I have done," she said loudly. "And I will not have you accuse me!"

"How can this be?" Eli answered. "How can you do such a thing? Is this plain? Is this the ordnung?"

Book lifted the globe on the lantern, blew it out, started to turn away . . . then sat down on the edge of the porch, and listened.

"I have done nothing against the ordnung," Rachel said, "and you are wrong to suggest it."

"Eh? Nothing? Rachel, you bring this man to our house. With his gun of the hand. You bring fear to this house. Fear of English with guns coming after. You bring blood and whispers of more blood. Now English music, and you are dancing to English music! And you call this nothing?"

"I have committed no sin," Rachel said.

"No sin? Maybe. Not *yet*. But, Rachel, it does not

126

look!" Then, in a softer tone. "Rachel, don't you know there has been talk? Talk about you, not him. Talk about going to the Bishop. About having you shunned!"

"That is idle talk."

"Do not make light of it, Rachel. They can do it, quick! Like that! And then, then I cannot sit at table with you. I cannot take a thing from your hand. I cannot go with you to meeting!" The old man seemed to gasp for breath. "Rachel, Rachel, you must not go too far, dear child!"

"I am not a child," Rachel replied stiffly.

"You are acting like one," Eli snapped.

"No. You are. And I will be the judge of my own conduct."

"No, you won't, Rachel! *They* will be the judge! And so will I, if you shame me!"

"You shame yourself," Rachel said coldly. "And I am going to bed before you make it worse."

"I am not the one!" Eli shouted. "You are the one!"

There was the slamming of a door, and Book knew that Rachel had departed the scene with a bang. He could hear Eli muttering to himself for a time, then footsteps on the stairs, then silence, and the dark.

Book stood for a time looking out at the barn, listening to the night wind in the trees. And the only images he could summon were those of Rachel's lush body moving toward him as she danced. Or tried not to dance. And he thought that he had never seen anything so appealing . . . had never seen any woman so sweetly and gently available. Like a faun, he thought, out at the salt lick just beyond the outer limits of her world, her tongue tasting, her eyes dancing, her heart pounding; knowing that the shot was about to be fired, and that she would fall, dreadfully hard, a guilty thing surprised.

Book snapped himself around, started across the porch toward the door. Book, old boy, he thought, time you were moving on. Time you stopped lusting in your heart, lousing up the lives of innocent people. So hear this. Tomorrow we will raise a barn, we will raise our wretched consciousness, and we will raise our lazy wounded ass back into motion just as soon as Stoltz-fus's tea will allow.

CHAPTER TWENTY-ONE

Schaeffer smiled across his desk at Carter, his eyes full of warmth and sincerity. "I just want to talk to him. Talk some sense into him. You know we go way back, Carter. You know we were a team once, just as you two are now. I trained John Book. And I love John Book. Now I know you're in touch with him." He held up a hand. "Don't bother to confirm or deny."

"I won't," Carter said flatly.

"Right, right, I know how it is with partners. All I'm asking is to talk to him. I *know* he's with the Amish." Schaeffer laughed, a forced, false laugh. "God, I'd give anything to see him now." He turned, smiling genially at Carter. "Can't you see John on his knees at a prayer meeting?"

"Why not?" Carter said. "He's got knees."

Schaeffer's genial expression slipped a bit, but he rallied, moved around the desk, sat on the edge of it, leaned toward Carter fairly wrapped in sincere concern. "Carter, listen. This police force, it's . . . it's a band of brothers. A team, a club, if you will, with its own rules. John Book has broken those rules. He has violated our code. He has to answer for that, just as you will, if you continue to protect him. Do you understand that?"

"No," Carter said. "But I understand something else."

"What's that?"

"I understand Book's going to take your white ass out, Paul."

And, as Schaeffer stared after him, Carter got to his feet and walked out of the office.

CHAPTER TWENTY-TWO

The Zook farm lay at the bottom of a lovely, tree-filled valley, the farmhouse set in the precise middle like a white teacup in the center of a perfect saucer. Coming down the slight grade toward it, Book thought he had never seen a prettier farm, and said so to Eli.

Eli, driving Tittle with obvious pleasure, shook his head. "No, Book, it is not so good when it rains heavy. Poor Zook gets floods. He don't sometimes get on his land until the middle of May."

"I'm not talking farming," Book said. "I'm talking pretty."

"You talk too much pretty, Book," Eli said.

Book gave it up, glanced around at Rachel and Samuel in the back. "Speaking of pretty," he said. "How's Oberg?"

Samuel shook his head. "She had a litter of five," he said. "Two of them brown, the other three mostly white."

"Fast Walpot," Book said.

"He really wanted to be a father," Samuel said.

"It's just the way with rabbits," Rachel said, matter-of-factly. "They can't help themselves."

Book nodded as his eyes met Rachel's. She held his gaze for a moment, then smiled a very small smile before she looked away.

They got into a traffic jam of buggies as they approached the Zook farm, and parked in a lot adjoining the barnyard in which at least thirty buggies were already neatly arranged. The Zook barn had been struck by lightning and burned to the ground, but all traces of it—except the original foundation—had been cleaned away. All around the foundation were piles and stacks of new lumber, and about three dozen men were already at work laying out the beams and studs of the new barn.

Book watched as Rachel, Samuel helping her, carried trays of doughnuts and two big baskets of other food toward the tables the women had set up under the trees. He looked to Eli, who handed him a satchel of tools. "What do I do?"

"Come with me. We'll ask the carpenter foreman for a gang you can work with."

"Book!" someone shouted. "Good to see you!"

Book looked around, and there was Daniel Hochleitner loping toward him, big hand and big grin extended.

"Hello, Daniel," Book said, putting out his hand. Hochleitner seized it and very nearly drove Book to his knees with his grip. "Easy, Daniel. I think I'll be needing that."

"Oh, sorry, Book. I'm just so happy to see you up and around again."

"Oh," Book said.

"He's a carpenter," Eli said.

"That's what Rachel just told me," Hochleitner said, with more enthusiasm than the situation seemed to warrant. "She said I should take you in hand."

Book nodded, thinking, The suitor is glad to see me up and around. The suitor will now take me in hand and make sure no harm comes to me. So that I'll be sure to get the hell out of the suitor's way at the earliest opportunity. Book smiled and said, "It's been a while."

"That's all right, Book," Daniel Hochleitner said, with a grin as big as his jaws would allow. "You come with me. You work in my gang, you won't need to worry."

"I think I can hold up my end."

"Your hole is healed then?"

"Getting there."

"Good!" Hochleitner whooped. "Then soon you can go home!"

And, as he put a long arm around Book's shoulders and led him off toward the foundations, Book couldn't help grinning, and thinking, Jesus, it's nice to be wanted.

It was a strenuous morning. It started as Book reported with Hochleitner to a gang nailing studs from the right-side roofbeams down to the first right-side uprights. Book took one look at the outline of the thing, discernible in the studs and timbers being laid out, and spoke to Hochleitner. "You don't really expect to put up a building of this size in one day, do you?"

"By sundown, Book," Hochleitner said, nodding his smile. "And it will last a hundred years, God willing."

He worked side by side with Daniel Hochleitner throughout the morning. And was very impressed with the man, his geniality and competence. Daniel Hochleitner was easily the best damned carpenter Book had ever clapped eyes on: an absolutely tireless driver of nails and spikes, and all of that driving done with an accuracy and speed that damned near defied the naked eye. What Book was not so impressed with was Daniel's almost nonstop eye contact with the concession stands (as Book called them) where the ladies manned the coffee and lemonade tanks, and where Rachel was prominently employed. Although Daniel never seemed to miss a nailhead, he also never seemed to miss a chance to catch Rachel's eye and give her a little wave without ever missing a hammer stroke.

By mid-morning, when Book—who was truly trying to be competitive with Hochleitner—allowed himself his first visit to the coffee table, he was beginning to get sourly annoyed. He took a cup of coffee from Rachel, and said, "How's your wrist?"

"What?" Rachel said. "My wrist?"

"Yeah," Book said. "Is it swollen?"

"Why should my wrist be swollen?"

"Well, with all those little waves to Hochleitner, I thought by now it'd be about the size of a summer squash."

Rachel looked at him thin-lipped and angry. "John Book, you are a stupid man. I was waving to you, as well."

"Is that right?"

"Yes, and I'll tell you what else is right." She leaned to him closely. "All of the ladies are saying that there is talk about me and the English." She backed away, nodded. "What do you think of that?"

"You and me?"

"Yes."

"What do *you* think of that?"

"I will not say."

"Well, are the ladies being charitable? I mean, do they think our intentions are honorable?"

"Almost none of them," Rachel said, grinning a bit.

"That's your ladies for you," Book said.

Samuel came up at this moment, looked at Book, and said, "You are doing good, they say."

Book smiled at Samuel, glanced at Rachel, nodded. "Never better, Sam."

"Samuel," Rachel said, correcting Book.

"I don't mind Sam," Samuel said to his mother. To Book he said, "I've been watching. You're keeping right up with Daniel. And he's the best. If it wasn't for your gun holes, I bet you'd be the best ever."

"Thanks, Sam. Samuel," Book said, glancing at Rachel again. "I'll try to hang in there."

And Book went back to work with a lift in his step, thinking for the first time about what life as a farmer would be like. Then he caught himself, and thought, What the hell *would* it be like?

By lunchtime, Book was beginning to flag. But so, as Book reckoned it, was Daniel Hochleitner. The Amishman was still driving nails and spikes true and fast, but not as many as before, and with not nearly the élan previously observed. Especially curbed were his glances toward the ladies. His glances now were mostly directed at Book. He would grin from time to time, but go right back to his hammering. And Book was damned if he'd give an inch. He worked until his sides and belly were screaming for relief, and when he did cross to the tables for lunch with the ladies, he was too sore even to think about food. He fell against a tree, allowed Samuel to bring him some iced tea, and only managed to wink at Rachel (much to her shock) as she passed among the men dispensing lemonade. But he charged right back to work with a springing stride when the eating ended, and he hammered nails, sawed beamjoints and drilled bolt-holes with resolute energy.

He started to flag again during the raising of the barn's framework. He joined in on a rope with about a dozen other men, including Daniel Hochleitner. It was a hard pull, the barn's end-beams heavy, the operation calling for a steady, even strain on the rope. Book started to black out when the framework was about halfway up, but he held on until the frame was in place and braced. Then he staggered away and sat down under a tree. Hochleitner followed him.

"Are you all right, Book?"

"I've been better."

"You don't look so good."

"I'll make it."

"I think maybe you should call it a day, Book."

"Oh, no. I'm in for the whole nine yards."

"But now we go up high. You should stay on the ground."

"You should see me when I'm high," Book said, grinning. "I'm the wonder of the world."

Hochleitner smiled. "You don't have to prove nothing, Book."

"Oh yes I do. I'm not sure exactly what it is, but as the single, only, official English on this here project, I've got to prove it."

"Because Rachel is watching?"

"Rachel . . . and Samuel," Book said, eyeing Hochleitner with new respect. "And I appreciate your frankness."

"You're a funny man, John Book. And a stubborn one. I got to keep my eye on you."

"You do that."

"I will. You stay close by me all the time."

"See you on the roofbeam," Book said jauntily.

And it was on the roofbeam, about three hours later, that Book almost lost it. True to his word, Hochleitner had insisted that Book work beside him. And, true to his, Book had insisted on working high. They were together at the top when it happened. Both were astride the double beam, facing one another, preparing to spike the beams together when the beams started suddenly to move apart, threatening (as Book described it later) to split them both up the crotch like wishbones. Book, caught with a spike in one hand and a hammer in the other, froze, and shouted, "Jump! It's going!"

"No," Hochleitner shouted, dropping his hammer. "Don't move!"

And Hochleitner leaned forward, wrapped one arm around each beam, and, with incredible strength, pulled them back together. "Now," he said, through gritted teeth, squinting up at Book, "spike it!"

"Yes, sir!" Book shouted, and drove two spikes home with great precision.

"Good job, Book," Hochleitner said. "You're some English."

"Who dropped the hammer?" cried an indignant man far below. "It almost hit Whitey Beiler in the head!"

"Don't say a word, Book," Daniel Hochleitner said, grinning at him. "Almost don't count."

Book collapsed against one wheel of the Lapp buggy, slid down it exhausted to the ground. He cocked one eye up at the roofbeam—probably forty feet in the air—and nodded. "That would've done it, Book. Broke your goddamned neck."

"Who are you talking to?" Rachel said, coming up from behind.

"My friend, God," Book said, peering up at her from under the brim of his straw hat.

She strode around in front of him, took a wide-legged stance, and put her fists to her hips. "Yah," she said, nodding her head vigorously, her jaw thrust out. "You should talk to God. Thank Him for not letting you kill Daniel Hochleitner. And yourself into the bargain!"

"Well, you took the words right out of my prayers," Book said. "By God, you don't miss a trick, do you?"

"Stop swearing, and no I don't. I was watching, and it was your fault."

"My fault? I didn't pull those beams apart."

"Your fault to be up there at all. In your condition. And Daniel's fault. And I will speak also to Daniel."

"You do that," Book said. "He's right over there." Book pointed to where Daniel was standing at a water bucket with a dipper in his hand. "Give him hell."

Rachel turned, started away, then looked back. "You stay right there. We're going home in a minute."

"Yes, ma'am," Book said. He thought, Brace yourself, Hocklight. Your comeuppance is on its way up.

That evening, after a bath in the washtub behind the kitchen stove, and after a dinner of one dill pickle (all he could eat), Book sat on the settle on the front porch exhausted, thinking that he was a bit further from a return to duty than he had figured. One hard day's work had left him drained, damned near destroyed. He looked out over the pond, listened to the night music of the frogs and the crickets, thought about Philadelphia —his apartment, his car, his office—and heaved a long sigh. Book, he thought, do not be a total damned fool. You are now resident in one of the best, safest rest homes in the known world. You have the respect and the warm solicitude of the proprietors, and even the interest of the beautiful lady who does the cooking. For once in your errant and eristic life, do the intelligent thing. Relax and recoup. And proceed very carefully with the beautiful lady. For we have here, Book, no lasting home. You'll never make a farmer, let alone an Amish farmer.

"Mr. Book?"

Book turned and there was Samuel standing at the door in his nightshirt. "Hey, Sam."

"I have a thing to say."

Book pulled himself upright. "What's that?"

Samuel stood for a moment, hesitating, then ran across the porch to Book, threw his arms around him. He held on for a long moment, then turned and ran back inside.

Book looked after him, then spoke softly, "Same to you, Sam."

Some minutes later, having almost nodded off, Book decided it was time to get himself to bed. He stood up, stretched, crossed to the door, entered and closed it behind him. And then noticed that there was still a light burning in the kitchen. He started down the corridor. "Sam?" he said softly. "That you?" There was no answer. Book moved on toward the kitchen, beginning to mutter about how household discipline was certainly going to hell around here, with people running off to bed leaving the lights burning. He was still muttering as he got to the kitchen door and looked in. And what he saw caused him to stop in mid-mutter and stare.

Standing by the kitchen stove dressed only in a white cotton camisole, Rachel was preparing her bath. She finished pouring a bucket of steaming water into the round tub (the same tub Book had used earlier), put the bucket down, pulled the camisole up over her head, and stepped naked into the tub. She stood with her back to Book, finished folding the camisole, set it on the floor by the tub, straightened again, and then appeared to stiffen. She stood perfectly still for an instant, then turned and looked straight at Book, presenting herself fully to his gaze. She met his eyes for a long moment—not boldly, but rather inquiringly—and then spoke very softly. "Well?"

Book—staring at her beautiful face and eyes, her strong breasts and loins—was rendered immobile, speechless. His mouth moved, but no sound came out.

Rachel ended the moment. Bending very slowly, she picked up the camisole, covered herself, and turned away.

Book backed off, turned, and moved back up the corridor shuffle-footed. And he thought, Jesus Lord God. And there I stood on hold.

PART THREE

CHAPTER TWENTY-THREE

Carter was already half dead when McFee and the three other officers dragged him into the warehouse. McFee rammed Carter up against a wall, held him there while one of the other officers unwrapped four nightsticks from a wadding of newspaper. He passed the clubs around, handed the last one to McFee. McFee thrust the end of the club up under Carter's chin.

"You see this, motherfucker?" McFee said. "We goin' to do you real slow. You don't tell us, this is goin' to take fuckin' hours."

Carter, rallying from somewhere close to unconsciousness, rolled his eyes around, looked at McFee. "You still here?"

McFee socked him back against the wall hard. "Don't you hear me, nigger? You tell me where that shithead is, or you're goin' down, all the way down!"

Carter somehow managed a tiny smile. "Fuck you, nigger," he said, almost sweetly. Then spat full in McFee's face.

The swat of the clubs went on for fifteen minutes

before McFee called a halt, and the four officers left. Carter lay on the floor on one side, his face streaming blood. After a moment, in the utter silence, a rat came out of the shadows and crouched down a foot from Carter's face. And held there, for a time, looking into the dead man's shining eyes.

CHAPTER TWENTY-FOUR

Book stood in the milkhouse door and watched as Rachel moved across the henyard, scattering feed to the chickens. She was dressed in cap and apron, and had her face tilted up to the brilliant morning sun with a small smile on her face.

Look at that, Book thought. One of the premier women of the world. Body, soul, and gorgeous face. And here I stand, tongue-tied. I am either the world's biggest damned fool, or else I am developing a conscience. In any case, I owe the lady a word of explanation. Or apology. Or whatever the hell.

He stood for a moment, unable to urge himself into motion and then walked toward her slowly, not knowing what he would say when he got there. She surprised him, keeping her eyes averted until he was almost to her, then snapping around and saying, "Well?"

"Well," Book said, slightly annoyed, gesturing with both hands. "What the hell?"

"Stop being profane," she said.

"Forget it," Book said, starting to turn away. "I thought I had something to say, but I lost it."

"You discourage very easily."

He turned back, eyed her closely. She was still smiling a very small smile. "If you're referring to last night, that wasn't it."

"I wasn't referring to last night," she said demurely. "But, since you bring it up, what was it?"

Book hesitated for a time, then said, "The rational process."

"Is that right? For a simple Amish woman, you have to explain."

"Okay," Book said, getting more and more annoyed. "If I'd made love to you, I couldn't leave."

She stared at him, losing her smile. "Of course you could. What kind of nonsense is that?"

"I mean . . . I couldn't leave as easily. Or readily. I'd have felt a sense of . . . obligation."

"You feel no obligation now?"

"Sure. Sure I do. But it'd be different. If I'd made love to you."

She looked at him evenly for a long moment. "I would not have allowed you."

Book nodded. "Well, I guess that settles that."

"You may be sure it does," Rachel said, snapping her eyes away from his and walking briskly away.

Book looked after her. Well, Book, he thought, there's your invitation to the dance. Now what the hell are you going to do about it?

Early that afternoon, Book sat on a bench outside the Strasburg general store waiting for a tourist to get off the public telephone. Rachel had initiated the trip into town, saying she had some shopping to do, and Samuel and Eli decided to go along to shop for a pocket knife and some vegetable seeds, respectively. Book wasn't going to go, when the trip was first announced, but the more he thought about it the more he thought it a good idea to give Carter another call. A progress report, nothing more. But essential that Carter be encouraged to keep the faith, hang in there until reinforcements arrived.

The tourist on the telephone was a large man whose volubility was only matched by his girth. Disgusting specimen, Book thought. The son of a bitch must eat twelve hours a day, talk the other twelve. And Book had just turned from a glance at the fat man when he was accosted, as he thought, by a lady tourist with an enormous camera.

She waggled it at him, and said, "Could I, I mean, would you mind if I—?"

"Lady!" Book said, interrupting. "You take my picture, I'll take your brassiere off and strangle you with it."

The woman fell back, gasping, trotted off hugely toward a tour bus. Samuel, seated on the edge of the porch a few feet from Book, drinking a Coke from a can, doubled over in laughter. Book grinned over at him.

"We Amish don't believe in graven images, right, Sam?"

"Right!"

"We don't believe in brassieres, either, do we?"

Samuel, gone in laughter, was unavailable for comment.

Book, frowning, listening to the number ringing, finally barked into the phone, "Answer, damn it! I'm a salaried employee!"

"Philadelphia police," said a female voice.

"Lieutenant Elton Carter, please."

"Just a moment, please." There was a clicking on the line. "I'm sorry, did you say Elton Carter?"

"That's right."

"Is this a member of the family?"

Book stiffened, barked again. "No, this isn't! This is his goddamned partner! What kind of a question is that?"

"Well, I'm sorry, sir, but Lieutenant Carter was killed last night in the line of duty."

Book pulled the phone away from his ear, stared at

146

the coin box for an instant. Then he put the phone back to his ear, spoke softly. "That's Elton Carter?"

"Yes, sir."

"You're certain?"

"Yes, sir."

"Thank you," Book said quietly. And he hung up crying, "Son of a bitch!"

"Marilyn?" Book said. "Is that you?"

"Why, yes. Who is this?"

"John Book."

"John, how are you?"

"I've been better, but I suppose I've been worse."

"I know the feeling. You want to speak to Paul?"

"If he's there, yes."

"I'll get him."

Book could hear Schaeffer's wife call to him, heard him say he'd take the call in the study . . . then heard Schaeffer say, "You can hang up, dear." There was a slight click, and Schaeffer said, "Is that you, Johnny?"

"It's me, Paul," Book said. "You pissant."

Schaeffer laughed nervously. "I like your style, Johnny. Calling me at home so I can't run a trace on the call. That's what I call style."

"That's what you *would* call style, you pathetic bastard."

"Don't be abusive, John. Don't make it worse than it is. We're close, very close. We know where you are. We're about—"

"Shut up!" Book snapped.

"We're coming after you, Johnny."

"No. You got it wrong, Schaeffer. I'm coming after you."

"Johnny, maybe if you come in we can work something out."

"We're going to work something out, Paul. First, I'm going to cut your fucking throat." There was a loud click on the line, the dial tone came on. Book hung up the phone, spoke softly. "And then, Paul, I'm going to do you some real damage."

The others had been waiting awhile when Book climbed into the buggy. "You look angry, Book," Eli said.

"I am angry," Book said.

"It's the telephone," Eli said. "That telephone will make anybody angry."

"I don't want to talk about it," Book said.

"When the little airplane crashed in the tobacco," Eli said, "they made me get on the telephone to tell the police, or maybe it was the newspaper. . . . Which was it, Rachel?"

"He doesn't want to hear about it," Rachel said.

"And I never got so angry in my life," Eli went on. "I told them—"

"Eli," Rachel said. "Nobody wants to hear."

"What's that?" Samuel said, pointing up the street.

"That is Daniel Hochleitner's mare," Rachel said.

"They have blocked him," Eli said.

Book looked up the street, saw where an Amish buggy was stopped in the one-lane street with a pickup truck stopped in front of it, heading in the opposite direction, blocking the buggy's passage. "What's the matter with those people?" Book said. "The pickup can back up to either side. The buggy's got no place to go."

"Daniel can back up," Rachel said. And, at the moment she spoke, a second Amish buggy came out of a sidestreet and pulled up behind the Hochleitner buggy.

"He can't back up now," Book said, watching as three young men piled out of the pickup truck and walked toward Hochleitner's buggy. "Let's get up there."

"But that will make three," Rachel said.

"Are you going, or do I have to walk," Book said.

"No need to shout," Rachel said, urging Tittle forward.

148

Book saw it coming, and when it began to happen, it happened very quickly. The three young men began to taunt and abuse Daniel Hochleitner. The Amishman simply sat and took it, even when one of the young men rammed a beer can into his face, telling him to have a drink. Then the young man—the apparent leader—knocked Daniel's hat off, stepped on it, and, taking an ice cream cone from his girlfriend, jammed it into Daniel's face.

Book departed the Lapp buggy the moment it stopped, with Rachel protesting, "No, John, it is not our way!"

"Right," Book said, as he started forward. "Be right back."

As Book arrived alongside the Hochleitner buggy, the leader was saying, ". . . get on down, you gutless wonder. If you ain't going to back up, you're going to get knocked on your ass."

"You are making a big mistake," Book said to the leader.

"What?" the leader said. "Well, Jesus God, look at this. Another one. You want your fuckin' face busted, too?" And, foolishly, he reached out and shoved the heel of one hand into John Book's face.

Book exploded, hitting the young man four shots to the face before he could so much as raise his hands in defense. He started down, spurting blood, and, Book hit him a fifth blow on the nose. The young man's nose burst like a ripe tomato, and he went down soughing like a spent wind. His girlfriend and two companions stared in disbelief. Book looked down at the young man, and said, "You learn some respect for your elders, boy, or you may get seriously injured next time."

"He broke his nose!" the girlfriend cried, rushing to the leader.

"You shithead!" one of the other young men shouted, far and away the biggest of the three. "I'll tear you a new asshole!"

Book smiled as he turned to meet the big man's

149

charge. He struck him two heart shots and another blow to the throat, and the big man went down gasping . . . sat down, suspiring, his eyes wide and startled.

"My God, Book," Daniel said. "I think you've killed him."

"No such luck," Book said, grabbing the third young man by the throat. "You go move that goddamned pickup truck before I hand you your fucking head."

"Yes, sir," the young man said. "Yes, sir!"

And the young man turned and ran to the truck, burned rubber backing it up and over into a parking space. Book turned to Hochleitner. "It was not worth all that, Book," Hochleitner said. "They are truly injured."

"Go ahead, Hochleitner," Book said. "They deserve to be truly injured." And without looking back at his victims, Book strode back toward the Lapp buggy. As he passed the second buggy, the Amishman driver looked out at him pop-eyed. "You are Amish from where?" the man said.

"Dark side of the moon," Book said, going right on.

"Must be from Ohio," the Amishman said to someone in his buggy.

Book climbed back into the buggy to stony silence. Until Samuel said, "Boy, they got a lesson!"

"Samuel!" Rachel said. "You will say nothing!"

"It does not look," Eli said. "You have hurt these men. It is not our way."

"Well," Book said. "It's my by God way, and that's all that need concern you. I take full responsibility."

"Oh sure," Eli said. "But they know this is Eli Lapp's buggy."

"I'll explain to the police," Book said.

"You may have to," Rachel said, as she urged Tittle forward. "Those young men are still sitting there."

"The hell with those young men," Book said, as they drove by them. The leader was being administered to by his girlfriend, and the other hadn't moved from his landing spot. "They're a discredit to the race."

"Mr. Book did what he had to do," Samuel said. "They might have hurt him."

"Be quiet, Samuel," Rachel said. "You know better."

"You see?" Eli said, "You see what happens? Now Samuel says it's good to hit people."

"No, grossfather. I said it's maybe sometimes necessary."

"No, Sam," Book said. "I did it because I was feeling mean, and I wanted to hit somebody. And that's the truth."

"Hey!" shouted a man, as they drove toward the near corner. "Who's that Amish? Never saw nothing like it in all my days!"

"He's my cousin from Ohio," Rachel said.

"Well," said the man, who was long, angular, and trumpet-voiced. "Them Ohio Amish must be different from ours! I mean, the local brethren don't have anything like that kind of fight in them!"

"He just lost control," Eli said. "He will be repentant."

"Is that Eli Lapp?" the man said.

"Never mind who it is," Book roared.

"That kid's nose is broken!" the man shouted back. "I don't call that never mind! How'd you like yours broken?"

"How'd you like a short punt in the tool bag!" Book shouted.

"Hush!" Rachel snapped at Book, and put the long whip to Tittle.

"This ain't good for the tourist trade, you know!" the man shouted. "I'm the former mayor of Strasburg, Eli Lapp! And I'll keep this in mind!"

Rachel whipped Tittle around the corner and out of earshot. No one spoke for a time. Then Eli said, flatly and simply, "We are disgraced. They may even send police."

Book stared at the road for a moment, then said softly: "If they send police, I will explain it all to them. Turn myself in, if necessary."

151

"That's very good of you, John," Rachel said. "If a little late."

"But what if they get nasty?" Eli asked.

Book almost groaned. And couldn't keep himself from his response. "Then I'll kick their dumb asses up into their eyebrows," Book said.

And he retired into himself and refused to participate in anything, including conversation, until well after milking time.

CHAPTER TWENTY-FIVE

The Undersheriff pulled his car up the street slowly, seeing the former mayor, Bill Ottenbrite, out in the street waving at him. He could also see the two young men sitting to one side of the street being attended to by the ambulance crew. He had heard all about the incident on the patrol car radio, but, not wanting to rob Ottenbrite of his reportorial privilege, he smiled as the ex-mayor came up and said, "What happened?"

"Damnedest thing I ever saw," Ottenbrite said, and then went on to describe Book's actions in fairly accurate detail.

"Don't sound like no Amish to me," the Undersheriff said.

"That's what I say," Ottenbrite trumpeted. "You don't expect that sort of thing from no kin of Eli Lapp!"

"Eli Lapp? He got a daughter named Rachel?"

"Daughter-in-law. The son got killed in a sileage chopper."

"Oh yeah," the Undersheriff said. "I remember. About six months or so back."

"I think you'd best check into this Ohio Amish," Ottenbrite said. "Don't need his kind around here."

"I'll surely do that, Bill. I'll surely do that." And the

Undersheriff drove up and stopped next to the ambulance, thinking: Have to call that asshole of a chief in Philadelphia. Just might have a nice lateral move here . . . get my ass out of Lancaster County. And, as he climbed out of the car and started toward the ambulance crew and the two young men, he was thinking about how he might just parlay the thing into a sergeant's appointment on the Philadelphia police department.

CHAPTER TWENTY-SIX

Book stood by lantern-light in the workshop, putting the finishing touches on the birdhouse. It had a new roof, a new perch, and now a new coat of paint. He had just decided that what it finally needed was a new trim job in red—and was sorting among the paint cans for a suitable red when Rachel came in. She looked at him sidelong, inspected the birdhouse, nodded, then sort of shrugged.

"You don't have to bother with the birdhouse," Rachel said. "If you're leaving soon."

"I'm leaving tonight," Book said. "I'm going to need my clothes."

Rachel looked at him, looked away. "Tonight."

"Seems like the right thing to do. After today," Book said, busying himself with a can of red paint.

"Never mind today. It can be forgiven and forgotten. But going back so soon, I don't like it."

"Where I'm going, I don't much like it either."

"Then stay a while longer."

"I can't. I've got things to do. Promises to keep."

"And nothing here?"

"No promises," Book said, somewhat defensively.

"You have not sought promises here," Rachel said.

Book hesitated, then nodded. "No."

"So," Rachel said, after a moment. "You will go back. To find them. To do what you did to those men in Strasburg. Only worse." She shook her head. "You are *gegewort*, a contradiction. So full of righteousness, yet so full of rage. And never thinking that it is God's place to take vengeance."

"That's your way, not mine."

"That's God's way."

"Well," Book said, a bit impatiently, "in the city of Philadelphia, God needs a little help."

Rachel stared at him, held the stare for a long moment, then looked away. "So, I will get your clothes ready."

"I'd appreciate it."

Rachel crossed to the door, hesitated, turned back, spoke very softly. "Last night, when you saw me in the kitchen, I . . . I tried to look for you the way I thought you would want a woman to look." She looked at the floor for a time, then spoke barely audibly. "I am sorry that I did not." And she went quickly out.

Book stood pole-axed, staring at the empty doorway. And what he felt, to his surprise, was an overpowering sense of loss.

CHAPTER TWENTY-SEVEN

Rachel stood at the ironing board trying to make Book's clothes presentable. She was using flatirons, which had to be heated on the cookstove, and, since it was a warm night already, the kitchen was almost a steamroom. The windows were wide open, and she kept dabbing at her forehead with a small towel and going to the nearest window for a breath of night air.

Through this window she was also watching the determined progress of Book's campaign to remount the birdhouse. Samuel and Eli were helping until she'd had to call Samuel in at his bedtime. Eli continued to help—putting in a new pole in the ground, fixing the birdhouse to the top of it—until it was too dark for Eli to see. He'd stood back for a time watching Book work, and just now had started toward the house, telling Book—shouting it, so that Rachel heard—to stop trying to gild the lily.

Eli came into the kitchen shaking his head. "That man is the worst *glotzkopp* I ever met!"

"What's he doing?"

"He says the pole isn't straight, so he's got to put guy wires on it."

"He's a driven man."

157

"He's a *glotzkopp*," Eli said, wiping his brow, and getting himself a glass of water. Then, noticing the heat from the stove, he said, "What is this, Rachel? You have to iron on a night like this? You are doing maybe penance?"

"Didn't he tell you?"

"Book? Tell me what?"

"He's leaving tonight. After the birdhouse."

"He is?" Eli nodded. "So?"

"These are his clothes."

"Oh. Well then." Eli sat down at the table. "So? Is he mended yet? He fights good, *Gott* knows. But I don't think he's mended."

"You want him to stay?"

Eli thought about this for a time, then shook his head. "No. He is strong. He will be just fine. And he belongs where he belongs. You know it and I know it."

"He is trying to protect Samuel, you know. After the fight today, he is afraid he has given Samuel away."

"He told you this?"

"No, but I know it is so."

Eli let the pause lengthen. "Rachel, you want him to stay?"

Rachel ironed fiercely for a moment, then said, "I am not sure."

"Rachel, Rachel, you know it does not look. He is not only an English, he is a police. You would really try to think he could be an Amish?"

Rachel turned, slammed a flatiron down on the stovetop, and spoke with annoyance. "I am not really trying to think!" she said. "Maybe I would go to Philadelphia with him! Why not?"

Eli's mouth fell fully open. "Rachel, you don't mean this!"

Rachel picked up a hot iron, turned and ironed briskly. "It is my life, Eli, and I will do with it what I choose."

"But . . . but your soul, Rachel. And Samuel's soul. What of that?"

"That," Rachel said, "is my business and Samuel's

business." She turned, clanged an iron down on the stove. "And God's. God's, Eli, not yours. Do not forget that."

"But, Rachel, what does this mean? You would leave us?"

Rachel banked the stove, pushed the irons aside, picked up the finished clothing. She started out without speaking to Eli, then relented. "You meddle, Eli. And you vex me. I don't know if I would leave you. But I will not leave you without careful thought. And giving of notice." She took a deep breath, sighed. "I am going to talk to John Book, take him his clothes. Please take care of the lamp."

"Yes, yes, I will," Eli said, nodding. Then, as Rachel started out, he spoke again, urgently. "Rachel, are there any nuts?"

Rachel stopped short, sighed, looked at him. "You know where the nuts are."

"No, no," Eli said. "I looked in the pantry, I couldn't find any."

Rachel heaved a definitive sigh of annoyance. She turned, set the clothing down on the table, looked at Eli, spoke shortly. "Come here, into the pantry. I will show you. Perhaps you are also going blind."

"No, no, I'd be grateful," Eli said, with uncharacteristic humility, getting to his feet immediately and following her into the pantry.

Rachel led him down to the far end of the narrow room. A room of shelves, all of them lined with Mason jars full of canned vegetables and fruits: tomatoes, beets, squash, beans, plums, peaches, pears, and applesauce. Rachel stopped at the end, pointed to the lower shelf on the right lined with small, plate-sized baskets full of nuts. Without so much as a look at Eli, she pointed from one basket to the next as she identified the contents of each. "Black walnuts, English walnuts, butternuts, Chinese chestnuts, filberts, pecans, shagbarks, and even some store-bought shellbarks." She turned to Eli. "And you couldn't find any nuts?"

Eli faced her, his old gray eyes clear and hard. "I lied

to you, Rachel. I just wanted to hear you say the names. I wanted to hear you speak proudly of your pantry."

Rachel glared at him. "That was very sly of you."

"I am sorry. But I wanted to remind you of what is the heart of an Amish woman."

"I did not need reminding."

"Yes, yes, you did, Rachel." The old man raised his eyes to the ceiling. "Rachel, Rachel, please tell me, what is happening?"

Rachel smacked her lips. "I think you are losing your mind."

"No. What is happening?"

"To what?"

"To the old ways?" He looked at her almost sweetly. "Why are you turning against the old ways?"

She started to answer, then sighed, sagged a bit, softened her tone. "I'm not turning against," she said, her eyes moving down the rows of Mason jars, her memory playing with all those hours of peeling and coring and snapping and steaming.

"Then what?" Eli asked, hanging over her.

"I'm turning toward," she said brightly, pushing past him, and walking out of the pantry. "Don't forget the lamp."

"No, I won't," Eli said, sounding confused, but more pleased than not. "Goodnight, Rachel."

"Goodnight, Eli," Rachel said, picking up the ironing and striding out of the room. "God keep you." And she marched out into the hallway with no clear idea of where she would go, or what she would do when she got there.

CHAPTER TWENTY-EIGHT

It was a spring evening, and yet it was a summer evening, soft and warm, the earth bursting with sound and seed and the sweet aromas of new life. Rachel stopped at the bottom of the pond and listened to the stream coming down and out through the waterwheel, a lovely, gentle gurgling; and she thought of the dozen years she had spent on this land, the plowing and the pruning and the picking and the putting up of the harvest in cans and silos and bins. And she thanked God quietly for all of those good and fruitful years, and asked another of Him. She made no mention in her prayer of what she was about to do. But she did ask God to take notice of her situation, and to please understand that even though the man was an English he was still a good and a stout and a formidable. And was even perhaps yet convertible to the true and single faith.

And, having listened for a time to the sounds of the night, and having delayed the business as long as she could, she tripped in a single jump across the stream, and went firmly uphill toward the birdhouse.

* * *

Book, when she found him, was kneeling on the ground twisting a guy wire. He cocked one eye at her and said, "I think I finally got it straight."

"I must talk to you," she said quietly.

Book looked at her, then looked back to the birdhouse. "From where you are, how does it look?"

Rachel gave it the most cursory of glances, then said, "It looks straight to me."

"Good."

"Did you hear what I said?"

Book, staring at the birdhouse, gauging its plumb-straightness against the night sky, didn't answer at once. But then, finally and slowly, he turned to her. "What you said? No, I guess I didn't hear."

"I said I must talk to you."

"Oh, right," Book said, getting to his feet. "I'll tell you something. This damned birdhouse has been driving me up the wall."

She regarded him solemnly for a long moment. "John, I don't want you to leave."

Book stared vacantly at the birdhouse for a moment, then turned, looked at her, hesitated, then said, "Duty calls."

"It will keep another week. Or two."

Book shrugged. "But why delay it?"

"I'll show you why," Rachel said, and she walked into his arms and kissed him on the lips.

Book pulled her to him gently, returned her kiss, then pulled away. "Are you sure?" he asked.

"I think I am very sure," and she reached up, pulled off her lace cap, and shook out her lovely long hair.

Book heard himself saying, "God."

And they made love there in the grass.

And when they were done, Rachel spoke only one word, "Stay."

Book didn't answer.

CHAPTER TWENTY-NINE

Schaeffer eased the green sedan to a stop at the top of the rise, looked down at the farm. "That has to be it," he said.

"Two ponds, two silos," McFee said.

"Let's go," Fergie said. "Sun's coming up."

The three men got out of the car, went around to the trunk. Schaeffer opened it, handed the two men short-barreled twelve-gauge pumpguns. They both filled their pockets with shells from two boxes in the trunk, then loaded the guns. Schaeffer took cartridges from a smaller box, poured them in his right jacket pocket, checked his revolver, nodded the others forward.

The morning mist was hip-deep along the driveway, and the three men went down through it toward the house looking alien and lethal. McFee and Fergie took opposite sides of the roadway, and the swirling mist almost concealed one from the other. Schaeffer, walking down the middle, said, "Slow up. The son of a bitch could be watching us right now."

"Well," Fergie said, "unless he's got a deer rifle, he ain't going to hit us from the house."

"Just slow up," Schaeffer said.

"Weird, man," McFee said. "No fuckin' electric poles."

"No fuckin' electric," Fergie said. "Not even underground."

"What do you figure they plug their shit into?" McFee said.

"They don't have any shit," Schaeffer said.

Rachel poured the bullets back into the cannister, then, almost lovingly, put Book's pistol up on the highest pantry shelf. And suddenly felt a small shudder of pleasure, and had to steady herself against a lower shelf. He had given her the pistol on his way out to the barn an hour before, and only then had she known that he would stay. And only then had she known how much it meant to her. If he had refused to stay, she thought, I would have had to go with him. And, standing there in the pantry, she realized—or allowed herself to realize for the first time—that she had fallen in love. She indulged the thought for a moment, then brought herself up short. Well yes, perhaps, she thought. But I must also consider John. It may not be the same for him.

"What?" Eli said. "What did you say?"

Rachel snapped around, looked to where Eli was sitting at the head of the kitchen table. The old man, who was not feeling well and was having an extra cup of coffee before going out to the barn, was looking at her in mild alarm. "I said nothing," Rachel said.

"You said 'John' and then you said something else," Eli said.

"Oh," Rachel said, coming out of the pantry. "I was just thinking out loud."

"I see you put up his gun. Is he then not going?"

"Not yet."

"So, he is going to stay."

"For now."

"Is that good?"

"I think so," Rachel said, moving to the sink, gathering up the breakfast dishes.

"You remember what I've been telling you, Rachel. He is not of us. He never would be."

"I don't know how you can be so sure," Rachel said. And it was at that instant that she saw the men coming up onto the front porch with the shotguns. "Oh my God!" she said.

"Eh?" Eli said. "What is it?"

"They are here!" Rachel shouted.

And, as she spoke, the kitchen door was banged open, and in came McFee and Fergie with their shotguns leveled. Schaeffer came in immediately behind them.

"Okay, people," Schaeffer said, pointing his pistol at Rachel. "Not a sound. It's Book we want. We're not going to harm the little boy."

"Get out!" Eli shouted, getting to his feet. "Get out of here!"

"Easy, old man," Schaeffer said. To Fergie he said, "Check out the rest of the house."

"You get out of this house!" Eli shouted.

"We're police officers. We're looking for a fugitive by the name of John Book. Is he living here?"

"He's not a fugitive!" Rachel shouted. "He is a good and faithful officer!"

"Right, lady," McFee said. "So he's here?"

"I did not say that!"

"Lady," Schaeffer said, trying to be smooth. "We're only here to enforce the law. John Book is a dangerous man. A criminal. An armed criminal." He smiled at Rachel, eased toward her. "He does have a gun, doesn't he?"

Fergie came into the kitchen. "He's not in this building, Chief."

"We're going to find him, lady," Schaeffer said. "You might as well tell us. It'll go easier on you, and might just save his life. You know about laws against harboring criminals, don't you?"

"John Book!" Eli roared, standing at one of the open windows. "John Book! They've come to kill you!"

McFee fairly leaped to where Eli was standing,

struck him a short, sharp blow with the butt of his shotgun on the side of his head. Eli swayed for a moment, then went down heavily to the floor.

Book, in the milkhouse, pouring milk from a bucket into a twenty-gallon can, froze at the sound of Eli's voice. He looked to Samuel, dropped the bucket, leaped across to the windows on the house side of the barn. He looked out and there was Fergie, moving out onto the front porch, shotgun in hand. Then the screen door banged and McFee came out to join Fergie.

Samuel, up beside Book and looking, said, "Is it them?"

"It's them, Sam," Book said.

"Have you got your gun?"

"No. It's in the house."

"What'll you do?"

"Never mind that, Sam. I'll tell you what *you* will do." Book turned, took Samuel by the shoulders. "Now, listen to me, Sam. Listen to me like you never listened to anybody before in your life."

"Are they going to kill you?"

"They're going to try, Sam. But they won't. Now listen to me! I want you to run across to Hochleitner's. Across the new corn. You hear me?"

"Yes, sir. And do what?"

"Just stay there. Don't do a thing."

"What are you going to do?"

"I'm going to take them out, Sam. You just do exactly as I say."

"Don't let them hurt you."

"I won't, Sam." He hugged the boy to him, then led him to the back door of the milkhouse, pushed him out. "Now, run, Sam! Fast as you can!"

Samuel, eyes big on Book, not wanting to go, said, "I wish I could help."

"You can, Sam! Just run! Run like hell!"

Samuel, wild-eyed, took off across the barnyard. Book turned and ran back to the windows. Fergie, proceeding cautiously, was about halfway to the barn, and McFee, quite as cautious, was just leaving the front porch. My goddamned gun, Book thought. Why did I have to give it back to Rachel?

He moved away from the window, crossed the cow stanchion area, and climbed a short ladder through a trapdoor to the upper barn. He ran to the car, thinking that, if he could get it started, he'd draw them into a chase, lead them to hell away from Samuel, Rachel, and the farm.

The car's engine turned over twice, then ran down to a grinding snarl. "Come on," Book said. "Just one time for daddy."

Fergie, a dapper man stepping carefully among the cowflops, stopped short as he heard the grinding of the engine. He turned to McFee. "He's trying to start a car."

"I can hear," McFee said. "You take the top part, I'll take the bottom."

Fergie nodded, moved uphill toward the upper barn. As he rounded the corner and headed toward the open barn door, the grinding stopped. Fergie checked the safety on his shotgun, moved forward very slowly. He eased around the doorjamb, peered inside. The car sat a few feet away from him, and appeared to be empty. Fergie put the shotgun to his shoulder, and walked in aiming. The car was empty. Fergie rechecked it, especially the floor of the back seat. And he was stepping back and looking to the rear of the barn when his eye caught a movement just behind the car. A quick, slight movement, over before his eye could intercept it. Fergie snapped around, gun leveled, walked the length of the car. A shaft of sunlight pooled on the floor almost under the rear bumper, and bits of hayseed floated in the brightness. Fergie stepped over, squinted at the floor. And saw the clear-cut outline of a trapdoor. "Book, you son of a bitch," Fergie muttered. "Stick your head up."

* * * *

Book stood at the head of a small passageway leading from the cow enclosure back past the entrance to the silo and around to the cow stanchions and the milkhouse. He was standing just inside the door, holding it slightly ajar as one cow in the enclosure was attempting to use the door to scratch the side of her head. He watched the ladder below the trapdoor he had just used to descend to the lower barn. He already had McFee located—now out in the cattleyard poking his shotgun into corncribs, feed sheds, and the hogpen—but Fergie needed watching.

After a long moment, a slanting of sunlight appeared at the top of the ladder, then the probing muzzle of a shotgun. Then one foot, then the other, and Fergie began to come down the ladder. The farm's resident goat went straight over and stared at Fergie as he came down the ladder. Fergie hesitated, then jabbed at the goat with the shotgun, and the goat grunted and backed away, took his stance about ten feet off, lowered his head, and glowered as Fergie stepped off the ladder into the enclosure. Fergie eyed the goat nervously.

Good goat, Book thought. Butt the bastard through the back wall. Book eased back as Fergie moved toward the workshop, took a deep breath. Lord God, he thought; there are men here out to kill me dead. Please do thou take my PPD ass into your divine care, Amen.

He started back along the passageway, past the door to the silo and then he stopped. He had attended a bit of work in the silo one afternoon with Eli, fixing an access door and a grain chute baffle at the top. He turned back, went toward the hatch leading to the silo, stopped just before he entered it, stood up, and grabbed the bottom of the ladder attached to the outside of the silo. He pulled himself up into the narrow, enclosed tube, finally got his feet on the rungs of the ladder, started up . . . and froze as he heard a door slam below him.

He stood motionless for a full minute before there

was a sound of movement in the passageway. Book hadn't thought it through, but he wanted Fergie in the silo. Just what he would do once he got him there was not clear, but he wanted him there. So he doubled his fist and beat three times hard on the side of the silo.

Then he waited, the sweat pouring off him, dripping off his hands onto the ladder. Waited a good minute and a half before Fergie—poking the muzzle of his gun before him—appeared in the crawlway below him. If he looks up, Book thought, I'm a dead man. Fergie didn't look up, but went on through into the silo.

Book immediately dropped to the ground, reached in, grabbed the access door's handle, said, "Goodbye, Fergie, you horse's ass," very softly (Fergie snapping around pop-eyed, meeting Book's eyes, struggling to get the gun around in time), and slammed the access door shut just as Fergie unloaded three shots into the other side of the door.

By which time Book was swarming up the ladder toward the top of the silo. He came out on the small platform at the top, looked down through the open trapdoor. Fergie was standing on the silo floor, reloading the shotgun. Book eased himself across the trapdoor toward the grain chute release, accidentally kicking a bit of grain down through the opening as he crossed. And he had no sooner cleared to the other side than Fergie fired three more shots straight up. The framework around the trapdoor splintered here and there, and Fergie shouted, "Book! Let me out of here or I'll blow your fucking ass off!"

Book moved to the operating handle on the grain chute. Eli had wanted to clean, and perhaps paint, the inside of the silo before filling it. But he felt Eli would understand, especially now as Fergie began to blast away at the access door. He'll blow it off, sooner or later, Book thought. And here I sit at the top of the goddamned ladder. "Goodbye, Fergie," he said aloud, and pushed the grain release handle forward.

The grain came rushing out of the chute, shot across within a foot of Book's face, and poured down into the silo with the roaring sound of snow in full avalanche.

Looking down, Book could see Fergie reloading again, staggering as the first smash of grain struck him and knocked him down, and firing from where he fell, emptying the gun. Fergie struggled to his feet, shouting something about Book, started to reload again. And went down again, the dust now almost obscuring him from Book's view. There was another salvo from the shotgun, then—just dimly seen through the dust by Book—there was Fergie clawing at the access door, then batting at it with the butt of the shotgun, then reloading again and firing into it as the grain climbed to his waist and above. Fergie was shouting nonstop now, calling upon God and McFee and Schaeffer to save him. And his mouth was open in full shout when the wheat came surging across the silo in a foot-high wave and silenced Fergie forever. He struggled, his left arm shooting up and the hand grasping for something solid to grip; then, fingers working, he sank beneath the next wave of wheat, and was gone.

Book, watching coldly, let the wheat pour down for another half minute, then reached over and shut the blower down. The noise of it gradually subsided. There was a moment of silence. Then, into it, came the roaring voice of McFee. "Fergie! You stupid little bastard! Where the hell are you and what are you shooting at?"

Book, starting down the ladder, muttered, "Come and find out, you murdering son of a bitch."

Rachel sat at the table next to Eli, handing him hot cloths to put to the wound on his head. Eli had sufficiently recovered to tell Schaeffer that he was an abomination unto the Lord, and that he would invariably burn in hell. Remarkably, Schaeffer seemed disturbed by the old man's vehemence, but had still refused Rachel permission to go look for Samuel. They were to sit right where they were, and Schaeffer stood there gun in hand to make sure that they did.

But then the shooting had started in the barn. Rachel had come immediately to her feet, started for the door. Schaeffer had ordered her back to her chair, putting his pistol in her face and cocking it to enforce it. Schaeffer had moved out to the porch as McFee shouted to Fergie, and moved further out onto the porch as he himself shouted: "McFee! Did he answer?"

"No!" McFee shouted.

"Well, what the hell's going on?"

"Why don't you come out here and find out, Chief!"

Schaeffer came back to the kitchen door, barked in at Eli and Rachel. "I'm going out to the barn. But if I see one of you outside of this house, I'll drop you where you stand. You hear me?"

"God hears you!" Eli shouted. "You spawn of the devil!"

"Just stay put!" Schaeffer said. "You stay put, lady, and no harm will come to your boy. I guarantee it."

"I guarantee your damnation!" Eli said.

Schaeffer shook a forefinger at Rachel, and moved away. When he had left the porch, Eli spoke quickly, quietly. "Book's not got his gun of the hand?"

"No. It's in the pantry. You saw."

"Then at least he's not shooting anybody."

"But it means he's getting shot at."

"Book knows shooting at. As long as it's not Samuel."

"It could be Samuel. For all I know."

"Book would protect him."

"If he had his pistol."

Rachel started to rise. "No, Rachel, you must not."

"Those men are trying to kill him. You can hear the shots."

"They could kill you, if you get in the way."

"I will take the chance, Eli!" she said fiercely. "For

171

Samuel. And for John Book." Eyeing Schaeffer—who was off the porch, moving very slowly, on his way to the barn—Rachel crossed toward the pantry.

"Rachel, Rachel," Eli said, trying to hold his voice down. "I can't let you do this!"

"Be quiet," Rachel said.

"It is not our way!"

"It must be done!" Rachel snapped. She reached up, took the holstered pistol down from the shelf, crossed to the stove, took the cannister down. She set the pistol aside, opened the cannister, spilled the bullets out on the counter. Eli had gotten to his feet, now came over to her, still holding a cloth to his head. Rachel, her hands trembling as she took the pistol out of the holster, said, "Don't, Eli. Don't interfere."

"We must find another way," Eli said. "Not a gun of the hand."

Rachel finally managed to find the chamber release, swung the chamber open, picked up a bullet. "What other way?" she said to Eli. "The way of the martyrs?"

Book tried the access door at the bottom of the silo, couldn't budge it. The wheat had sealed it shut. He looked up, went to the ladder, climbed to the second access door. It gave a little, but was warped, wouldn't open. Need a hammer, Book thought. Maybe a crowbar. He dropped down the ladder, went cautiously out into the passageway.

"Fergie, you little fucker!" McFee shouted from the upper barn. "Where the fuck are you?"

Thank you, McFee. Had to get you located. Book went to the door of the cow enclosure, eased it open, went across the open space ducking from one cow to another, hiding finally behind the goat just in front of the workshop. As Book hesitated, the goat lifted its tail and evacuated its bowel. Book staggered away into the workshop, thinking, My God, goat. I speak well of you.

172

He selected a crowbar, a hammer, a huge screwdriver, and, as an afterthought, a short-handled maul. He eased out of the workshop, moved carefully toward the open trapdoor leading to the upper barn. He listened for a time, set himself, then tossed the maul up through the trapdoor, heard it clang loudly against something, and sprinted back toward the silo as McFee opened fire above with his shotgun.

McFee fired toward the sound with great accuracy. The maul had struck the rear axle of the Lapp buggy, and McFee proceeded with five rapid-fire shots to shred the top of the buggy, blow the dashboard off, and leave the backscreen hanging by a thread. McFee ducked behind a hayrake, reloaded, and shouted, "Come on out, Book. I know you're hot! You want to shoot, I'll shoot with you!"

There was only silence. And the silence lengthened because McFee, knowing Book, had no intention of taking him on one on one. And, after a moment, he turned and shouted, "Schaeffer, you gutless wonder! Get your ass out here!"

Samuel had run all the way to the Hochleitner farm and had found no one there but the ninety-three-year-old great-grandmother. She smiled, offered Samuel some milk and berry pie, and was finally persuaded to reveal that Daniel and the rest of the family were working a field they rented on the Yoder farm, just to the far side of the Lapp woodland.

Samuel had turned and started back, and had gotten just opposite the main barn when the shooting started. He stopped short, knowing that they were shooting at John Book, and knowing that John Book did not have his gun.

He hesitated for a long time, hiding behind the crown drill, wondering what he should do. His mother and Eli were in danger, and so was Book. And he was able to help. He knew he was able to help.

And he was still hesitating when he heard five shots, and heard somebody shouting, challenging Book. Samuel took off at top speed, holding his hat, holding his pace as befitted the best runner in his school, swinging down across the tobacco toward the old wheat field so that he could approach the house from the west. He thought, as he ran, Dear God of us, keep my mother and Eli and John Book from gun holes, Amen.

Rachel had loaded all but one bullet, had dropped that one and was retrieving it from the floor, when Schaeffer suddenly shouted in at the kitchen door. "Hey, what the hell are you doing?"

Rachel, concealing the pistol in her skirt, straightened up slowly. "I dropped my eyeglasses," she said, not turning around.

"Well, find them and let's go," Schaeffer said. "You're coming out to the barn with me."

Rachel looked at Eli, eased the pistol up onto the kitchen table, the chamber still hanging open. She quickly removed her apron, covered the pistol with it, turned toward Schaeffer. Eli was getting to his feet when there came a voice from the back of the room.

"Momma?"

Rachel and Eli turned to see Samuel standing at the window that opened on the spring house. Rachel started to speak, but caught herself just as Schaeffer stuck his head in the door. "Let's go!"

Rachel and Eli hurried toward the door . . . but Eli, happening to see the farm bell on its crossbeam just behind Samuel, paused long enough to make the motions of a bellringer in violent action. Samuel looked pop-eyed at Eli, then caught on, looked around at the bell, turned back to Eli and nodded. Eli immediately turned, hastened to join Rachel at the kitchen door, looked out at Schaeffer and said, "And not only that, you will burn in hell for all eternity! No release, you know? No mercy!"

And again Schaeffer looked disturbed as he herded Rachel and the old man toward the barn.

Book looked back from the cow enclosure door, saw McFee's boots at the top of the trapdoor ladder. He ducked back into the passageway, closed the door, fastened it, and went in to the silo ladder. He climbed up to the second door, started to work on it. He pried, poked, hammered—could not get it open. He gave up after a moment, dropped to the lower door. Just two whacks with the hammer, and the door backed away into the unpacked sileage. He leaned on it, suddenly found it breaking off of its hinges. He twisted it, pulled it out of the aperture, tossed it aside. Wheat poured out rather steadily, but Book climbed right in, knowing that its level was not more than two feet over the aperture. He found Fergie's body almost immediately, and the barrel of the shotgun clutched in one of Fergie's hands. Standing hip-deep in the soft wheat, Book checked the weapon, found it empty. He plunged back to the corpse, eyeing the access door the while, found Fergie's jacket pocket, pulled out two shells, loaded them into the shotgun. And he had no sooner worked the slide and looked back toward the access door than he saw McFee's face in the aperture, staring in. McFee leaped back. Book leaped forward, hitting on his belly, the shotgun muzzle thrusting through the access door. Book fired twice as he landed, and kept sliding forward and came to rest with his chin against the threshold of the access door.

So that he saw what happened to McFee. Struck full in the chest by both shotgun blasts, McFee was driven six feet backwards and came to rest dead on the floor just outside the cow enclosure.

Book crawled to his feet, ducked through the access door, walked out toward McFee's body. And stopped short as he saw, off to his left, Rachel, Eli, and Schaeffer. Schaeffer was holding his pistol to Rachel's head, and he said, "Drop it, Johnny, or I'll blow her head into small pieces."

Book, still holding the empty shotgun, dropped it. And said, "Schaeffer, you hurt these people, I'll peel you like a fucking grape."

And, at that moment, there came the sound of a bell, clanging rapidly, from out in the direction of the main house.

CHAPTER THIRTY

The big bell was ten feet up in its cupola, and Samuel was lifting three feet off the ground with every lift of the rocker arm. It was the biggest and best bell in the district—well-known for its sound and power—and Samuel was clutching the rope and riding it as if it were a bronco's bridle. So that he had, literally, to be seized and plucked from the rope by Eli when the old man came up behind him.

"It's all right," Eli said. "Well done, Samuel."

"Where's Momma, where's Book?" Samuel said.

"They're coming, with the last one," Eli said.

"The last one?"

"Book killed two of them," Eli said. "God help him."

"God help them," Samuel said immediately. "But what's to be done?"

"Look," Eli said, pointing. "You already did it."

Samuel turned, looked off toward the woodlands. And there they came, at a trot or steady walk . . . the Amish. Daniel Hochleitner and his brothers, Stoltzfus from beyond them, and even Fisher the Mennonite . . . all coming to answer the sound of the bell, the Amish cry for help.

* * *

They came out of the barn with Rachel walking ahead, and with Book behind, and Schaeffer holding his pistol to Book's head. The Amish were already walking in from all sides as Schaeffer forced Book up the drivewa y toward his car. And there came a moment, quickly, when the Amish had blocked the road and surrounded Schaeffer, Book, and Rachel.

"What is this?" Daniel Hochleitner said. "What are you doing to John Book?"

"He is a criminal," Schaeffer said, eyes darting side to the side, already amazed at what was happening. "I'm a police officer, a chief of the Philadelphia police. I've come to arrest him for murder. And he just murdered two more men, in the barn. Now, get out of my way."

"You have a warrant for his arrest?" Daniel Hochleitner said. "If you have a warrant, we would like to see it."

"I didn't have time for a warrant! Now get the hell out of my way or I'll shoot him right here!"

Daniel Hochleitner folded his arms. The other Amish, taking Hochleitner's lead, closed in around him. Eli thrust himself in to stand next to Daniel.

"Get out of my way or I'll shoot!"

"You can't shoot all of us," Eli said.

There was a moment, as Schaeffer glared around, adjusted his grip on his pistol, and watched the Amish move in, closing the circle ever more tightly. A moment when it appeared he was actually going to start shooting.

But then Book spoke, very quietly. "Put the hammer down, Schaeffer," he said. "It's over."

"You shut your fucking mouth!" Schaeffer snarled. "You did it all! You're the one who caused—"

Book wheeled, quick as a bobcat, and took Schaeffer at the pistol with one hand, at the throat with the other, and forced him, throttled, to his knees. He snapped Schaeffer around, choke-locked him, tossed the pistol into the henyard, snatched Schaeffer's handcuffs from his belt, and handcuffed him with the ease and efficiency of a street officer who was demonstrating technique to a police academy class.

"Now," he said, "I place you under arrest for complicity in the murder of Officer Peter John Zenovich. And in the murder of Lieutenant Elton Carter. Both of the Philadelphia Police Department! And any attempt on your part further to resist arrest will result, I assure you, you pissant, in your instant death!"

Book grabbed Schaeffer up from the ground by the cuff chain, swatted him forward with the heel of his hand to the back of Schaeffer's head, and started him up the driveway toward the green sedan. But, in that moment, his eyes caught Rachel's. And she looked at him with an expression somewhere between shock and dismay, and he knew that Schaeffer's career was far and away the least of those things that had just ended in that particular barnyard.

CHAPTER THIRTY-ONE

Book took Schaeffer directly to the District Attorney's office, and found his friend, Assistant District Attorney Doyle Bendix, on duty and quite disposed to listen. It turned out that the District Attorney had been tipped by an informant as to the perpetrators of the Zenovich murder, and had already traced possibilities back to McFee, and thence to Paul Schaeffer. Schaeffer was immediately booked on suspicion, and Book's assurance of an entirely reliable witness of the murder of Zenovich by McFee was accepted on its face value. Affadavits were prepared by Book as to the incidents at the Lapp farm in Lancaster County, and these were signed and witnessed hours before the first reports began to come in from the Lancaster County Sheriff's Office.

The matter of the murder of Elton Carter was also discussed. Neither Book nor Bendix had any doubt as to the principal perpetrator. But, since he was already dead, Book asked Bendix to delay any further investigation until he, Book, could return to full duty in Internal Affairs. Whoever helped McFee were no doubt police officers, and Book said he wanted all the time he could be allowed to develop leads and evidence. He wanted no least chance of mistake in the pursuit and identification of the murderers. Bendix granted the request, asking only about the delay. Book said he had unfinished business in Lancaster County.

Bendix, looking at Book's Amish garb, said, "Right, John. And give my regards to God."

CHAPTER THIRTY-TWO

Book came out of the house feeling slightly odd in his street clothes, with Eli behind him making reassuring remarks. "You look awful in them clothes, Book," Eli said. "But you looked worse in Amish."

"Thanks a lot, Eli," Book said. "Where's Samuel?"

"Down there," Eli said, pointing toward the waterwheel. "He wants to be a police."

"He'd make a hell of a police," Book said. "But he'd make a better Amish."

"You tell him that," Eli said. "You show him your holes!"

Book walked down to the pond, sat down by Samuel. "Hey, Sam. How's the race?"

"The race?"

"For salvation."

Samuel stared at Book for a moment, then looked away. "Yeah. I guess that's what it should be called."

"What?"

"Life."

Book nodded. "About as close as you'll get."

"Do you like being a police, Mr. Book?"

"No."

"Then, why do you do it?"

Book thought for a moment, then said, "Salvation."

Samuel looked at him closely. "Yes," he said, "I can see that."

Book smiled. "I'll be seeing you in a few months, Sam. You'll have to come into court in Philadelphia."

"I know," Samuel said. "Momma told me. I don't mind."

"Good."

"But . . . you're not ever coming back, are you, Mr. Book?"

"No, Sam," Book said, getting to his feet. "Just isn't in the cards."

"What cards?"

"It's an English expression, Sam. Hard to explain."

"Yes," Samuel said, nodding. "That's the trouble with most English things."

Book, finding nothing suitable to offer against so incisive a comment, took Samuel in his arms, hugged him quickly, and walked away, saying, "See you in court, Sam."

Rachel was waiting on the porch when Book came up from the pond. She smiled, came toward him with a black hat in her hand. "I have a thing for you."

Book looked at the hat, then at Rachel. So lovely a woman, he thought. And so far the reach. He smiled. "Waste of a good hat," he said.

"It is for remembering."

"I'll remember," Book said. "I don't need the hat."

"You left it under the birdhouse," Rachel said.

Book took the hat from her, put it on his head. "Hell," he said, "in honor of that, I'd wear the damned birdhouse."

He kissed her then, and she looked up at him with tears in her eyes. "Goodbye, John Book. Keep a close walk with God."

Book nodded, turned toward the car, and might have made it without sagging if Eli had not cried out, "Goodbye, Book! You be careful out there, among them English!"

Book drove up the driveway and was not especially

surprised to encounter Daniel Hochleitner, inbound in his courting buggy, at the top of the rise. Book shouted to him out the car window: "Hey, Hochleitner! I'll be back next week. To see to business!"

Daniel Hochleitner looked at him, waved, and shouted, "To see to what?"

"The coming of the Lord!" Book shouted, and drove on, looking back at Hochleitner and thinking, Go, Book. Go and keep going. You and God got other wars to fight.

EPILOGUE

CHAPTER THIRTY-THREE

That night when the house was still Rachel took a lamp into the spare bedroom and sat down by the bed. The Amish clothing Book had worn was hanging on hooks on the wall, and his high-top shoes were on the floor beneath them. Someday she would put them away. But not yet. Someday she would understand what it all had meant to her. But not yet.

One thing was clear: she was changed. And changed for the better. She had wanted, in the beginning, to get away. To get outside of Lancaster County, outside of being Amish. And to look back, and seriously to consider whether or not she wanted ever to return. And her idea had been that she would choose not to return . . . that she would find the outside world very much to her liking, once she had seen it.

Well, she had seen it, and it was violent, it was shocking, it was heartbreaking. She was sure there were good people among the English, church-going, well-disposed people. Even Book's sister, Elaine, had a good heart. But how, in the name of the living God could they live the way they lived? How or why? Without land or closeness to the land? Without a truly close walk with God? What was more important than these things? How did the English lose sight of what was really necessary to happiness? It was a mystery. But out of it had come, to her, a certainty: she was unalterably, irrevocably Amish. And she thanked God for that. She thanked God that she would now have the good sense to marry Daniel Hochleitner, in good time, and live the rest of her life with him. Here, on the good earth of Lancaster County.

As for John Book . . . she would never forget, would never be able to forget. For there was no doubt in her heart that she loved him, loved him as she had never loved any other man. Another mystery. They had made love, and she had never taken more deep delight in it—in her own body, or the body of another. But that wasn't why she loved John Book. She loved him for his bravery, for his humor, for his commitment to justice, for his brave and steadfast spirit. For his resolute refusal to allow the people of evil to stride over the English world.

He would be back, to take Samuel to court, and back again after that. And she was resolved to let him know, again and again, that she loved him, that her heart was now and forever with him. There would be in this no betrayal of Daniel. What was between John Book and her would only be of the spirit. But it would endure— she knew that—and she knew that it would nurture John Book as it would nurture her for as long as they both should live.

Preserve him, dear God, she prayed. Keep him from pain, from shots in the night, from gun holes in his body. Preserve him, sturdy God, for his own sake, but also for the sake of gentle people not so tough and strong as he is. For the gentle people need his lion heart to stand against the malefactors. And, dear Lord, never was there more of a lion heart.

She rose, took up the lamp, and started out. At the door, she turned back and finished her prayer aloud: "And, dear God, preserve him in his whacking. For in that there is none better."

And then she went out.

THE SEDUCTION OF PETER S.
by Lawrence Sanders

Peter S. was not corrupt from birth.
Childhood, adolescence, early manhood, he'd made the usual compromises, was never some pure and spotless moral paragon. But he'd been a pretty reasonable human being.
The corruption came later.
Too long in New York, struggling too long as an out-of-work actor, he was past the point where he could afford to be fussy. The job on offer would pay and pay well.
He'd been trained as a performer and one performance is much like another. Like a moral tranquilliser, a little luxury would soothe away all doubts.
So the corruption began and grew, eating away at him.
Others noticed. Outraged, his girl friend rejected him. Friends edged away. The professionally, criminally corrupt began to gather round him. The Mob was interested ...

NEW ENGLISH LIBRARY

THE YOUNG LIONS
by Irwin Shaw

Hailed as 'the outstanding novel to come out of World War II', *The Young Lions* begins during the troubled peace of 1938, and follows the fortunes of three very different men through the six tumultuous years to come.
Noah Akerman, trying to prove his manhood in a world gone mad, clutches at a forbidden woman and a destiny he dare not imagine.
Michael Whitacre, desperately trying to retrieve his self-respect, squanders his talents in a world of glitter and glamour.
A born hero, Christian Diestl is handsome, fearless, and never takes no for an answer.

'The finest of all novels of the last war ... unlike Norman Mailer, Irwin Shaw does not reduce his soldiers to the sub-human level; all the time we see them dually, both as fighting men, and ordinary citizens. We recognise them. We know their faces.'
Daily Telegraph

'Packed with incident, with credible versions of Berlin as the bombs fall, and the morale crumbles, of desert warfare brilliantly illuminated, of simple love ... of social history and human courage ... Engrossing and heartening.'
Tribune

'Brilliant! Leaves the reader with a deeper understanding of the present world. No novel can be asked to accomplish more.'
New York Times

NEW ENGLISH LIBRARY

**Give them
the pleasure of choosing**

Book Tokens can be bought
and exchanged at most
bookshops in Great Britain
and Ireland.

BESTSELLERS FROM NEL

The Young Lions	*Irwin Shaw* £2.95
The Case of Lucy B.	*Lawrence Sanders* £2.50
The Seduction of Peter S.	*Lawrence Sanders* £2.50

CRIME FICTION FROM NEL

Death Bed	*Stephen Greenleaf* £1.95
Grave Error	*Stephen Greenleaf* £1.95
State's Evidence	*Stephen Greenleaf* £2.50
Money Men	*Gerald Petievich* £1.50
One-Shot Deal	*Gerald Petievich* £2.50
Captain Blood	*Michael Blodgett* £1.75
Hero and the Terror	*Michael Blodgett* £1.75
Quick Change	*Jay Cronley* £1.95

All these books are available at your local bookshop or newsagent, or can be ordered direct from the publisher. Just tick the titles you want and fill in the form below.

NEL P.O. BOX 11, FALMOUTH TR10 9EN, CORNWALL

Postage Charge:

U.K. Customers 55p for the first book plus 22p for the second book and 14p for each additional book ordered to a maximum charge of £1.75.

B.F.P.O. & EIRE Customers 55p for the first book plus 22p for the second book and 14p for the next 7 books; thereafter 8p per book.

Overseas Customers £1.00 for the first book and 25p per copy for each additional book.

Please send cheque or postal order (no currency).

Name ....

Address ....

....

Title...

While every effort is made to keep prices steady, it is sometimes necessary to increase prices at short notice. New English Library reserve the right to show on covers and charge new retail prices which may differ from those advertised in the text or elsewhere.